Dear Reader,

I'm often blown away by stories of everyday heroism many people display in facing enormous obstacles in life. Coping with a condition like renal failure requiring dialysis is huge and I know there are many people who struggle and succeed, just like the heroine of my story, Holly.

If you are one of them, you have my heartfelt admiration. And I wish, that just like Holly, a heroic person will appear in your life with the courage and the heart to give you the precious gift of health.

In Holly and Ryan's case the donor-recipient bond provided a rocky testing ground for a much deeper relationship. I got so involved with these characters that giving them the ending they both deserved was particularly satisfying.

Happy reading,

Alison Roberts

The
Surgeon's
Perfect Match

Alison Roberts

TORONTO • NEW YORK • LONDON
AMSTERDAM • PARIS • SYDNEY • HAMBURG
STOCKHOLM • ATHENS • TOKYO • MILAN • MADRID
PRAGUE • WARSAW • BUDAPEST • AUCKLAND

ISBN-13: 978-0-373-06564-6
ISBN-10:   0-373-06564-7

THE SURGEON'S PERFECT MATCH

First North American Publication 2006

CHAPTER ONE

THE tremor was tiny.

So slight it could only be felt, not seen, but it was enough to threaten her confidence.

Could she manage this?

The smallest slip could be catastrophic. A tiny heart lay carefully exposed beneath her fingertips. The defect causing a three-year-old boy's heart failure was visible and ready to be covered by the small teardrop-shaped patch of Dacron caught between the teeth of the forceps that surgical registrar Holly Williams was holding.

The tremor could be the result of first-time nerves, in which case Holly knew she could conquer it and succeed— as she had done countless times already on the totally focussed journey that had brought her to precisely this point in time.

But it could also be the result of fatigue and, no matter how much practice Holly had had in battling the physical effects of exhaustion, she knew there were times when she simply couldn't win. And the notion of a three-year-old child sharing the repercussions of losing that battle was absolutely unacceptable.

Pushing herself this far might have been a huge mistake. What if...?

'You *can* do this, Holly.'

The quiet, deep voice was so close that Holly could feel the vibration of air as clearly as she'd felt that embryonic tremor. And the confidence that had cloaked the words didn't stop at her ears. It seeped instantaneously into her brain and then swept further. The ache in Holly's calves subsided, the knot in her stomach unravelled just enough and her fingers felt rock steady.

She gave a single, decisive nod.

Of course she could do it. She had worked far too hard for far too long to pass up the opportunity of actually touching her dream.

Being more than an assistant, however vital that assistance might be.

So what if this procedure was an almost routine repair of one of the most common types of a 'hole in the heart'—a ventricular septal defect? Or that all the skilled preparation had already been done by one of the country's foremost paediatric cardiac surgeons? It was still Holly holding the suture needle and patch. Doing an actual repair herself and not just the final closure for the open heart surgery. There weren't many consultants in any field that would trust their registrars enough to provide such an opportunity so soon.

She owed it to her mentor to justify that trust. As she had done on more than one occasion when Ryan Murphy's confidence had deepened, if not actually engendered, an equal trust in herself.

'Begin on the right side of the inferior rim.' Ryan's instruction was calm. 'And carry it in a counter-clockwise direction to penetrate the septal leaflet.'

Tiny stitches. Through the cardiac tissue and then through the edge of the patch. Again. And again.

'Perfect.'

The final suture was tied and cut. The rush of oxygen as Holly took a deep breath gave her momentary dizziness. How long had she been holding her breath?

'Want to carry on?'

Holly glanced up to catch a pair of hazel eyes regarding her over the edge of a surgical mask. Ryan's tone was as calm as ever but Holly could see a gleam of pride that was bright enough to more than replace an emotion she couldn't afford to indulge in just yet.

'Yes—thanks.'

'Don't thank me. I'm getting a holiday here.'

As if. Ryan was aware of every factor involved in this operation. Coaching and monitoring Holly's work would require far more effort than doing it himself, and Ryan was also keeping tabs on all the parameters being measured on their small patient as the procedure was completed and preparation made to come off bypass.

'Clamp coming off. Happy that you've removed all the air in the aorta, Holly?'

'Yes.' Holly moved to insert the needle into the largest chamber of the heart, the left ventricle.

'Good.' Ryan nodded. 'You've got it right on the apex.'

The pause as the team watched for the heart to resume pumping stretched on longer than seemed normal and Holly felt a chill race up her spine. It was rare these days for defibrillation to be needed to restart the heart. Had something gone wrong?

Her gaze was riveted on the child's heart, still lying motionless, but Holly was aware of a very subtle movement beside her. The tall figure that had already been standing close beside her seemed to sway an infinitesimal degree. Not enough for anyone to notice but Holly was aware of Ryan's shoulder almost touching her own. The solid wave of reassurance the almost-touch provided coincided with the first movement of the tiny heart in her line of vision.

Just an uncoordinated wiggle to start with but it was enough for a collective, if inaudible, sigh of relief as the heart settled into a steady beat with reassuring swiftness. Then the whole chest moved as ventilation of the child's lungs began again. Step by step, Holly continued the procedure, repairing the connection sites for the heart-lung machine, positioning drains and closing the small chest with fine wire to hold the edges of the breastbone together. She had used virtually all these skills previously but never continuously, and the strain was telling as the final layer of closure was reached.

The tremor was clearly visible now.

Not that Ryan offered to take over. Not even when it took two attempts to knot and tie the final suture. His clipping of the excess length was perfunctory as his attention turned to the anaesthetist.

'How're we looking?'

'All good. Blood pressure's fine. Oxygen saturation is ninety-eight per cent.'

'Probably the best it's ever been for this wee chap. Happy to move, Holly?'

Holly finished covering the sutures with a clear plastic dressing and scanned the chest drains. There was no sign of any untoward blood loss from the field of surgery.

'I'm happy if you are, Ryan.'

'Oh, I'm more than happy.' They could all hear the smile in Ryan's words. 'Well done, Holly.'

'Yes, well done!' The sentiment echoed amongst theatre staff who were quite aware of what a large step Holly had just taken towards her ultimate goal of being a paediatric cardiac surgeon. The congratulatory sounds stayed with her as they transferred their small patient to the intensive care unit where he would stay on a ventilator for the next twenty-four to forty-eight hours.

She *had* done well but her clumsiness at the end of the procedure couldn't have gone unnoticed. How many of the staff were thinking, as Holly was, that it was just as well it hadn't occurred earlier? Or that maybe Ryan was a little *too* trusting. Worse—that maybe Holly Williams wasn't quite up to doing the job she had set her heart on.

Having directed them towards bed position one in the ICU, the charge nurse gave Holly a look that confirmed her fears.

'You look dreadful, Holly! You're as white as a sheet. Are you all right?'

'I'm fine.'

'Hmm.' But the nurse's attention was now on her new admission as they positioned the monitoring equipment and checked all the information made available. 'Callum's parents are in the relatives' room,' she told Ryan finally. 'You can send them in to sit with him when you've had a talk.' She raised her eyebrows. 'I'm assuming everything went well?'

'You'd better ask the surgeon.'

Holly smiled at the new level of respect she could detect in more than one face turning in her direction.

'It went very well,' she said modestly.

'Textbook perfect, actually,' Ryan added. 'Let's go and give Callum's parents the good news, shall we, Holly? We might even have time for coffee before we do our rounds after that.'

'Don't bank on it,' the nurse warned. 'I've heard that the neonatal retrieval team have been sent out to collect a blue baby from one of the maternity hospitals.'

'What's the ETA?'

'Thirty minutes or so, I'd guess.'

'Cardiology up to speed?'

'They're standing by.'

Holly listened to the exchange with dismay. An afternoon of patient rounds evaluating their current case load had seemed manageable, but if she was already drained enough to have people commenting on her appearance, how could she hope to find the stamina to assist with what could be a very difficult procedure on a critical newborn baby?

'In that case…' Ryan's tone belied any similar misgivings he might be having. 'Coffee is imperative. Holly, would you go and put the jug on, please? I'll talk to Callum's parents.'

'But—'

'No "buts",' Ryan said sternly. 'I need coffee stat!'

He could have been the one to go ahead to the staffroom while Holly spoke to the child's family but they both knew why that wasn't happening and it was with a heartfelt sigh, a few minutes later, that Holly sank into an armchair and closed her eyes.

Sometimes, this was just *so* hard.

His registrar was sound asleep.

Ryan Murphy shut the staffroom door quietly behind him when he arrived nearly an hour later. He'd spoken at length to Callum's parents and then accompanied them to their son's bedside, taking the opportunity for another check on his patient. He'd caught up with the cardiology team as their new admission had arrived via ambulance. The neonate was in trouble all right, with a level of cyanosis obvious enough to require urgent management. An X-ray and echocardiogram would be needed to make a definitive diagnosis, however, and that gave Ryan some breathing space.

It was time for coffee.

Maybe it was also time to have that talk with Holly.

She hadn't stirred as Ryan had entered the small staff-room. Before long, the area would start being used by staff snatching a lunch-break, but for the moment it was peaceful and Ryan was reluctant to disturb Holly. Exhaustion was etched onto that pale face in the form of an uncharacteristic frown line between her eyes and bruised-looking skin beneath the fan of dark lashes.

He'd never seen her asleep like this before and for a long moment Ryan felt mesmerised. That aura of strength had deserted her and the sheer vulnerability of the woman in front of him caught and squeezed Ryan's heart painfully. She was way too thin now. In another life, with Holly's height and stunningly good looks, she could easily have been a model. But that was not what Holly had set her heart on being, was it?

Ryan sighed inaudibly and moved towards the bench. He shouldn't have pushed her to go solo on that VSD repair. He'd seen that moment of hesitation—the self-doubt. He'd also felt the gathering of whatever internal re-sources had been needed to succeed, and he hadn't realised how tense he'd been himself until Holly had moved to take that first stitch and he'd been able to breathe again.

Not that he'd doubted for a moment that she could do it. If sheer courage and determination were all it took to succeed, there would be no stopping Holly Williams. Sadly, that wasn't all it took, though, was it? And Holly was getting just a shade too close to the wall now. Maybe others hadn't noticed yet but Ryan had become so closely attuned to his registrar that he knew as well as she must how much more of a struggle it was all becoming.

Yes. Ryan quietly set two mugs onto the bench and reached for the jar of instant coffee.

It was definitely time for the talk.

'Holly!'

Her eyes flew open at the sound of her name. Blinking, Holly focussed on the source of the sound. Shaggy, gold-streaked brown hair. A face too craggy to be conventionally good-looking but a pair of the kindest hazel eyes in existence. A wide mouth, more inclined to curve into a slow smile than a grin. The kind of smile she could see right now, in fact.

'Feeling better?'

Holly nodded, sitting more upright as she noticed the steaming mug of coffee Ryan was holding out for her.

'Thanks.' Embarrassed at being found asleep, Holly avoided more than the briefest eye contact. Her gaze slid past Ryan's face, catching the wall clock visible just behind his shoulder. Her exclamation was horrified.

'Oh, my God! I've been asleep for an *hour*!'

'You needed a rest.'

'I thought you'd only be five minutes. I only sat down to wait for the jug to boil.' Holly shook her head in disbelief, pushing a long, single braid of dark hair over her shoulder. 'I'm so sorry, Ryan. This is awful!'

'It's no big deal. Don't beat yourself up over it.'

'Falling asleep on the job is a pretty big deal in my book.' Holly tried to stamp on a fear that had been gnawing at her for days. The fear that things were getting worse far too rapidly to control now. That she was reaching a point when she would have to admit defeat. She could only hope that fear wasn't showing in her eyes as she looked up at Ryan again. 'Why on earth do you put up with me, Ryan?'

The gentle smile broadened into the closest he ever came to grinning as he sat down beside Holly.

'What is it they say on the wrinkle-cream ads? "Because you're worth it"?'

'Ha!' But Holly couldn't help smiling back at Ryan. He'd always made her feel like that. Mind you, he made everybody feel like that. His small patients, their parents— even their siblings. Ryan was just one of those amazing people that made anyone they spoke to feel special. Holly had never known him to complain of any personal cost he suffered and she had to be running up a fair account by now. 'You have to juggle on-call rosters because half the nights I'm unavailable. I have more time off work than any normal registrar would be allowed and now I'm falling asleep on the job, for heaven's sake!'

'You had a big morning.' Ryan raised his coffee-mug in a salute. 'Well done again, by the way. When I think back to what my first patch was like on a VSD, I'm impressed all over again. In fact, I think I was only allowed to do half of it before my consultant muttered darkly about having to call in a plumber to fix the leaks and then took over.'

'I don't believe that for a minute.' Holly's glance at Ryan was very direct. 'Why *did* you let me do it?'

'Because you could.'

'You didn't know that. *I* didn't know that. I've never done it before.'

'You have more than enough ability. You've got to stretch your wings some time.'

'But something might have gone horribly wrong.'

'Of course it could. Something could have gone horribly wrong for me as well. That fear is always there.' Ryan's expression was quizzical. 'You've had your heart set on a surgical consultancy for as long as I've known you, Holly. And that's, what…two years now?'

She nodded. 'Off and on.'

'And as a consultant, you take that risk and responsibility on board and do the best you can. *Your* best is more than good enough.'

'I'm not talking about the risk of complications or error.' Holly stared into the depths of her coffee-mug. 'I'm talking about the lack of physical ability. What if I'd blacked out or got the shakes badly enough to create a disaster?'

'You didn't.'

'You took a hell of a risk, though, Ryan.' Holly swallowed hard. 'And while I'm enormously grateful, I don't think you should do it again.'

'That's my call.'

Holly shook her head sadly. 'I'm not so sure about that. Not any more.'

'What do you mean?'

'Maybe it's time I faced reality here. The odds are stacked pretty high against me getting where I want to go.' Holly took a deep breath. This was hard to say. To admit that her fiercely defended independence wasn't as great as she'd believed. 'Maybe it's just not fair that people like you have to keep propping me up.'

Ryan was giving her an oddly wary look. 'You've been battling those odds for as long as I've known you and I've never heard you come even within spitting distance of admitting defeat. What's changed?' He frowned. 'Did I put too much pressure on you this morning? If I did, I'm sorry, Holly. I never meant to—'

Holly shook her head again, interrupting any apology. 'It's not that. You've never put too much pressure on, Ryan.' She smiled. 'You seem to know how to put on just enough to push people into discovering what they're capable of without destroying their confidence. You're a brilliant teacher, you know.'

Ryan shrugged off the compliment. 'So what is it? Are you just tired?'

'I'm always tired.'

'What's changed, then?' Ryan persisted. Hazel eyes seemed to darken with concern. 'Are you needing dialysis more often?'

'Probably. I'm due for blood tests today.' Holly eyed the remains of her coffee. Should she use up that much of her daily fluid allowance now or save it for later? She took another small mouthful and then sighed. 'I'm doing it four nights a week already, Ryan. Soon all I'm going to be doing is coming to work and going home to sleep with a machine.' She tried to throw in some of the customary humour with which she had always lightened such conversations. 'I really shouldn't tick the single box on forms, should I? I've had a partner for years.'

Ryan didn't appear amused. 'It's a temporary relationship. You know that a normal life will be entirely possible when you get a kidney transplant.'

'Yeah.' Impossible to keep her tone light now.

'That's it, isn't it?' Ryan looked as though he wanted to slap his forehead for being obtuse. 'That's what's changed. I *thought* you brushed off that disappointment last month rather too easily.'

Holly couldn't deny it. 'It's caught up with me now. To get *that* far…' The disappointment cut more deeply than ever right now. 'I kept telling myself it was better to have the plug pulled then than to go through the surgery and then have to wait to see if the transplant would work and then battling rejection and dealing with failure and the knowledge that another transplant would be that much more difficult, but I was kidding myself. To actually get prepped for surgery and then sent home was awful.'

'The donor kidney was found to have kidney disease that hadn't been diagnosed, hadn't it?'

'Yeah. Polycystic. Same as me. Ironic, eh?'

'No.' Ryan reached out to cover Holly's hand with his own. He gave it a brief, gentle squeeze. 'Incredibly disappointing. You'd waited so long.'

The empathetic touch would have been enough to generate tears in someone other than Holly, but Holly Williams had never cried about her illness. She had simply got on with the most important things in her life and refused to even consider letting it slow her down. Until now, anyway.

She touched the second pager she wore clipped to her pocket. The one that had only sounded once in all that waiting time. 'It's been more than two years,' she said quietly. 'I went on the waiting list as soon as I had to start regular dialysis.'

'You haven't fallen off the list,' Ryan reminded her. 'You'll still be at the top. A compatible organ could come up any time.'

'With my blood group? I'm O, Ryan—but in my case that's not really O for ordinary.'

He smiled. 'I could have told you that.'

Holly's smile in return was wry. 'I'm a universal donor but I can only receive from another O. And that's just the blood group. There's tissue and cross-matching factors to complicate things as well. Which reminds me, I'm due to send in the monthly sample today. Could you draw some blood for me later?'

'Sure.' Ryan had finished his coffee but he made no move to get up. In fact, he had a rather determined look on his face. 'I'm glad the subject's come up, actually, Holly.'

'Oh?' He was going to agree with her, wasn't he? Had Ryan just been waiting for an opportunity to ease her out of her senior registrar position?

'Yes. I've been giving your situation quite a lot of thought recently. Ever since that hiccup with the transplant last month.'

Holly waited, her heart sinking. He did want her to give up trying to work full time. He'd supported her so much for so long and the ace up her sleeve had always been that it was worthwhile because when she got her transplant she would make up for any inconveniences she had caused. They would never have such a committed and hard-working registrar on their team. Now Ryan could see, as she did, that holding out for the miracle a transplant could provide might be just a dream. The odds of it happening before she deteriorated further or even died suddenly seemed much smaller.

Almost non-existent.

The door to the staffroom opening at that point to admit one of the ICU nurses was a reprieve that Holly grasped with alacrity.

'Sue, hi! How's Callum doing, do you know?'

'He's good.' The nurse sat down and opened a packet of sandwiches. 'What are you two doing in here? I heard there was a blue baby on its way in.'

Holly's gaze swerved to Ryan. 'That baby must have arrived ages ago. Why haven't we heard anything?'

'I popped down to see her before while you were…getting the coffee. Sorry, I should have told you.'

Holly could feel the muscles in her jaw tighten. No. She should have been there as well. 'So what's the story?'

Ryan stood up, taking Holly's coffee-mug to the sink along with his own. 'Full-term baby girl. Nothing abnormal noted on foetal ultrasound. No murmurs but a loud second heart sound and she was still cyanosed on a hundred per cent oxygen.'

'Transposition of the great arteries?'

'That's our pick for the moment. They've probably done the echocardiogram by now. Shall we go and see what they've found?'

'Cool.'

Back to business as usual was fine by Holly. She was regretting having let the conversation become so personal. Her warm smile at Sue as they left the staffroom was, in some part, thanks for interrupting before Ryan had been able to ease into the subject of firing her, and Holly made sure their communication was purely professional as they threaded their way through the busy corridors of the large children's hospital.

'We don't get a transposition very often, do we?'

'Fortunately, no.'

'Surgery won't need to be immediate, will it?' The physical demands of the rest of Holly's day were suddenly looking rather more manageable.

'No, but it's usually done within the first week or two of life, before the left ventricle becomes unable to handle systemic pressure. If it's severe enough, they'll need an interim measure to improve the cyanosis.'

'A Rashkind procedure?' Holly had no difficulty in sounding more than interested.

'Ever seen one?'

'No.' Any residual despair at having her own physical weakness demonstrated so recently was chased away by excitement. 'I'd love to, though.'

'How much do you know about it?'

'It's designed to allow the systemic and pulmonary circulations to mix, isn't it? They thread a double lumen catheter into the left atrium via the umbilical vein. A balloon gets inflated with contrast medium and then pulled back through the atrial septum to create a tear.'

'Mmm. Strange business, this, isn't it? We spend half our morning repairing a septal defect and our cardiologist colleagues might well spend half their afternoon creating one.' Ryan was smiling at Holly. 'I take it you'd like to go and watch if it goes ahead?'

'Oh, could I?'

'Absolutely. Good learning experience for you. To be honest, I'd quite like to go and watch myself.'

'What about rounds?'

'We'll fit them in. We've got a consult to do in the ward as well. Another VSD who's developing pulmonary hypertension.'

'How old?'

'Eighteen months.'

'Is that Leo?'

'Don't tell me you've seen him already?'

'Not as a patient. He's been in the ward for a few days, though.' Holly's smile was a little embarrassed. 'He was part of that hide-and-seek game you caught me playing yesterday—when I should have been writing up those discharge notes.'

'You stayed far too late yesterday catching up on them. It's no wonder you're tired today.' Ryan paused as they reached their destination of the neonatal intensive care unit. 'And we're giving ourselves a very busy afternoon.' He held Holly's gaze. 'Are you up to it?'

'I'm not about to fall asleep again, Ryan.' Damn, this could provide another lead-in to that talk Holly really didn't want to have. Her chin came up. 'Of course I'm up to it.'

It was a struggle, anybody could see that, but there was no way Holly was going to admit defeat. She'd push herself until she fell over, Ryan observed with concern. No matter how hard it might be, she simply couldn't help herself going the extra mile.

Like the way she sat with baby Grace's shocked parents and drew them a diagram of what had gone wrong with the development of the arteries in their infant's heart because they hadn't been able to take it in the first time around with the cardiology team.

'So the aorta, which takes the blood from the heart to the rest of the body, is attached to this part of the heart on the right side, do you see? And that's where the pulmonary artery should be. So it means that the blood that's getting the oxygen from Grace's lungs isn't getting to the rest of her body, which is why her lips and fingers look so blue.'

Grace's father looked desperate to both understand and find a way to help his family. His tone was belligerent.

'It *can* be fixed, though,' he demanded. 'That's right, isn't it?'

Holly's smile both accepted the anger being directed at her and gave reassurance. 'When we operate, what we'll do is attach the arteries to the ventricles they should be attached to.'

'Why can't you do that right now, instead of that thing with the balloon they were talking about?'

'It's a major operation. We need to make sure Grace is strong enough and there are a few more tests we'll need to do before surgery.'

The baby's mother sat hunched in a wheelchair beside the incubator, her face pale. 'Can I stay with her?'

'Of course you can. The nurses will show you how you can help care for her. The procedure this afternoon shouldn't take too long.'

'Will you be there?'

'Yes. Don't worry, we'll all take very good care of Grace.'

Donning a lead apron so that she could stand close enough to touch the baby during the procedure in the catheter laboratory instead of observing on the screens in the technicians' area meant that Holly put ten times as much effort into that session than she needed to, but Ryan wouldn't have dared suggest that she took things easier.

His registrar was already building a bond with both this tiny patient and her parents that would make the upcoming surgery less traumatic for everybody. That kind of bond was automatic when Holly was involved. The huge grin she got from Leo when they slotted that consultation in during their ward round was another example.

The toddler sat on his mother's knee initially as they

examined the child, which wasn't all that easy because she was heavily pregnant. It was Holly who listened to his heart. She showed Leo the end of her stethoscope before approaching him. She wiggled it. 'This is Silly Snake,' she told Leo. 'He likes tickling people and he wants to wiggle under your T-shirt. Shall we let him do that?'

Leo nodded, wide-eyed.

'Wiggle, wiggle,' Holly whispered. Leo giggled as she positioned the disc. She listened intently for a full minute and then nodded. 'Wiggle, wiggle,' she said again, and she must have tickled the small boy as she removed the instrument because Leo writhed in mirth. It made both his parents smile and suddenly the consultation was far more relaxed than it might have been.

'What could you hear, Holly?'

'There's a harsh systolic murmur,' she reported. 'A pulmonary systolic ejection and a mitral mid-diastolic flow murmur. The pulmonary second sound is loud.'

'What does that all mean?' Leo's father asked.

'They're abnormal heart sounds,' Ryan explained, 'which we'd expect after the results of the catheter test Leo had yesterday. As you already know, that hole in the ventricular septum hasn't closed nearly as much as we would have hoped by this stage.' He glanced up at the X-ray illuminated on the wall of the ward's small consulting room. 'Leo's heart is increasing in size quite dramatically and so are his pulmonary arteries. We don't want that to continue. He's getting more symptoms now, too, isn't he? Despite his medications being increased?'

Leo's mother nodded. 'Ever since he started walking. He gets breathless very easily and he's always so tired.' She caught her husband's gaze. 'We were really hoping to avoid the surgery, though. Especially just now, with the new baby coming.'

'When are you due?'

'I'm thirty-six weeks now. And I may need a Caesarean. The baby's breech. They're talking about a procedure to try and turn it next week but there's no guarantee it'll stay that way. And if I have a Caesar it'll make everything that much harder, and if Leo's not well I just don't know how I'd cope.' She bit her lip and her hold on Leo must have tightened enough to transmit her tension because the toddler stuck out his bottom lip and wriggled determinedly free.

He went straight to Holly and held up his arms. 'Wiggle, wiggle!'

Holly grinned and a moment later Leo sat in her lap, happily playing with the end of her stethoscope. His mother watched him for a moment, fighting tears, and then she looked at her husband and they both smiled again.

The message was very clear. Holly had won their son's trust. Who were they to argue?

Ryan was equally reassuring. 'If Leo has his surgery now, he'll be a lot less of a worry by the time the new baby arrives. Kids bounce back from this kind of surgery astonishingly well. He'll be up and running around within just a few days.'

Details regarding the necessary surgery were discussed and consent forms even signed, with no hint of further tears, and Ryan knew that his registrar was largely responsible for leaving the small family relatively happy to settle back into the ward and ready to face the biggest hurdle in Leo's life so far.

They finished their afternoon by checking Callum's progress again in the intensive care unit. While Holly went through the process of reviewing every parameter and noting their satisfactory levels, it was clear she was at the very end of her physical tether.

When they turned to leave, Holly seemed to lose her balance. She swayed on her feet and might well have fallen if Ryan hadn't taken a firm grip of her elbow. Thank goodness he'd been standing so close.

It was a momentary lapse. Holly pulled free a second later, probably before anyone else had noticed what had happened, and she walked ahead of Ryan as they left the unit. He said nothing until they were alone in the corridor but something did have to be said. This was the opportunity Ryan had been waiting for.

'My office,' he commanded. 'We have to talk, Holly. Now.'

Holly sat amidst the clutter of stacks of journals and case notes in his office, looking as though an axe was about to fall, and Ryan realised that she was expecting some kind of rebuke for her physical failings. It was time she knew just how far from the truth that was.

'You're amazing, you know that?'

A flush of colour stained her cheeks. 'Maybe I'm just stubborn. I don't like giving up.'

'I'm not talking about the way you cope physically, Holly, although, God knows, that's extraordinary enough. I'm talking about you professionally.'

'You mean this morning? In Theatre?'

'No.' Ryan had to smile. 'But, there again, your talent as a surgeon *is* pretty outstanding.'

Holly looked nonplussed and Ryan's smile faded. He cleared his throat. There was a lot he'd like to say right now but this wasn't the time or place. He knew he had to tread very carefully here.

'I'm talking about the rapport you have with people,' he said. 'The way you can win their trust and calm their fears. You have a natural ability to deal with aspects of patient care that no surgical techniques or drugs could ever hope to touch. I suspect a lot of it has come because of what you've had to go through yourself but it's a gift, Holly. An art. One that needs to go hand in hand with science to achieve the kind of patient outcomes we strive for.'

'Um…' Holly seemed lost for words. Then she gave an embarrassed chuckle. 'Gosh, Ryan—this wasn't at all what I was expecting you to say.'

'What were you expecting?'

'That you were going to say that a career as a surgeon and living on dialysis were just not compatible. That my physical limitations were becoming way too much of a burden.'

Ryan nodded slowly. 'You were right. I am going to say that.'

It didn't seem possible for Holly's face to become any more pale but it must have done to make those dark eyes seem so huge. Ryan had to grit his teeth against the pain he knew he was causing.

'But I wanted you to know where I was coming from *before* I said that,' he explained gently. 'For you to know just how highly I value you as part of my team. And that, if I can help it, I have no intention of losing you.'

Her face was utterly still, her head held high on a long, slender neck. Ryan could see the ripple of muscle as she swallowed with apparent difficulty.

'I have no intention of losing me either.' What started

as a valiant smile went distinctly wobbly around the edges. 'What do you suggest?'

'A transplant,' Ryan said promptly.

Her breath came out in a huff of something very close to despair. 'Yeah…right. I'm working on it. See?' She held up a hand, the fingers crossed. Her words had a faint and alien ring of bitterness. 'Not much more I *can* do, is there?'

'Yes,' Ryan contradicted calmly. 'There is.'

Holly stared at him as though he was speaking a foreign language. 'Like what?'

'Like considering a living donor for a transplanted organ instead of a cadaveric one.'

Holly shook her head wearily. 'I've been down that track as far as it goes.'

'And?'

'And nothing. My mother died when I was ten, from the same kidney disease I have. My father's diabetic. My brother's not interested. Or, rather, he could be but he has a morbid fear of hospitals and illness and he's avoided talking about anything to do with my kidney disease ever since I was diagnosed.'

'What about other relatives? Friends?'

'I don't have any other close relatives and it's certainly not something I'd ask a friend.'

'What if the friend didn't need to be asked? If they offered?'

'It's not exactly minor surgery, Ryan, having a kidney removed. It would be taking a risk with their own life and future health with no guarantee that it's going to have the desired result. Who would put themselves through that?'

'Somebody who cares.'

Holly snorted without mirth. 'The last person that was

supposed to care couldn't wait to get away as soon as I had to start dialysis. Even if I'd had the energy to try another relationship, I doubt that I would have taken the risk.'

'I know someone,' Ryan said quietly.

A curious stillness settled onto the small room that was Ryan's office. The busyness of the hospital on the other side of the closed door could have been worlds away. Sounds that had already been muted seemed to fade away so much that the proverbial pin would have dropped with a clatter. Holly's whisper sounded weirdly loud.

'*Who?*'

Ryan Murphy licked suddenly dry lips. He leaned forward a little, closing the gap between them, and held Holly's wide-eyed gaze with his own, as carefully as his hands would have cradled a newborn infant.

'Me.'

CHAPTER TWO

How could a single word be that stunning?

The shock was enough for Holly to be aware of nothing but the echoes of that word reverberating in her brain. Her head swam and she closed her eyes.

Breathe, she told herself implacably. Do *not* faint in front of your boss. Do not make his impression of your physical capabilities worse than it already is.

Nothing had ever been this unexpected. This unsettling. Certainly not the diagnosis of the illness that had brought her to this point in her life. Holly had been monitored carefully from the moment her mother had been found to have had an advanced case of renal failure and her own deterioration to the point of needing dialysis had been far too slow to shock her. Holly had finished medical school and launched herself into a meteoric rise to senior surgical registrar status before that had happened. Even her brother's horror at the idea of being approached as a donor hadn't been unexpected, given how badly he'd coped in the final stages of their mother's illness.

But this… That one word suggesting that Ryan Murphy was prepared to offer one of his own kidneys was so far out of left field, Holly had nothing on which to anchor her reaction. It was, simply, stunning.

Ridiculous but stunning.

She had no idea how much time had passed before she opened her eyes again. Seconds? A minute or more? Nothing had changed. Ryan was still watching her with an expression she couldn't read. Compassion was there, of course, but it always was to some degree. What she couldn't pin down was what was mixed in with it. Hope? No, that couldn't be right. Resignation was more likely. Something had to be done about Holly Williams and this was Ryan just trying to help her out—yet again.

And now Holly had to fight not dizziness but the threat of tears, and as a form of demonstrating weakness they were just as unacceptable as fainting would have been. Holly closed her teeth over the soft tissue on the inside of her bottom lip hard enough to cause pain. She could taste blood but it worked. The prickle of tears was conquered. She even managed a smile.

Ryan raised his eyebrows. He smiled back, a shade tentatively as the silence dragged on, and Holly knew she had to say *something*.

Nothing sprang to mind.

'I don't know what to say,' she was forced to admit.

'Say yes,' Ryan suggested quietly.

Holly looked away. 'Have you got any idea what you're offering here?'

'Of course I do. I'm not stupid, Holly.'

There was an edge to his tone that Holly had never heard before. Ryan was offended.

'Sorry.' Holly raised her gaze to find that Ryan appeared not to have moved a single muscle. He sat like a statue, his gaze still fixed on her. 'It's an incredibly generous offer and I'm stunned, but it's totally impossible to even consider.'

'Why?'

Why, indeed? Because it was simply so huge. It was like, Holly thought wildly, an eccentric millionaire calling in his housekeeper, say, and offering to give her his entire fortune. A gift that would enable her to live the kind of life she'd always dreamed of.

Except that this gift wasn't money. It was a body part. Something so personal, the thought of even considering acceptance made something within Holly cringe in agonised embarrassment. But how on earth could she tell Ryan that without causing further offence?

'For one thing,' she said carefully, 'it's highly unlikely we'd be compatible. As I told you, my blood group is O.'

'So's mine.'

'So are forty-five per cent of the population, Ryan. But I'm not rhesus positive. I'm negative. That takes it down to seven per cent. One in sixteen people. Unless the situation is desperate, they're not going to go for anything less than a perfect match.'

'I'm O negative.'

Holly couldn't afford to let that tiny ray of hope in. This was ridiculous. 'And then there's tissue and cross-matching. It can look like a perfect match and then they put it together and get some horrible rejection reaction.'

'We're compatible, Holly,' Ryan said calmly. 'I've already checked it out.'

'*What*?' This was another surprise. Another disturbing one.

'I've had the initial tests done already.' Ryan sounded almost smug—as though he was producing his trump card.

'Doug said that if I'd come in dead I would have been considered a perfect match for you.'

'Doug?' Holly needed to confirm what she was hearing here.

'Your renal physician,' Ryan said unnecessarily.

'You've been talking to Doug about this…behind my back?' Holly's tone was measured, perfectly calm, but Ryan blinked, clearly disconcerted.

'Well, I didn't want to make an empty offer.'

'So you've ticked all the boxes and got it all planned.' Holly was still trying to assimilate the astounding information. 'Have you talked to anyone else about this?'

'I…ah…had a word or two with a transplant surgeon, just to see how much time off work I'd need to organise.'

'And?'

'Two or three weeks max. Less if it's done with keyhole surgery. No heavy lifting for six to eight weeks but that's not a worry with our jobs. I reckon we could both be back on deck within three weeks.'

'You didn't pencil in a date for surgery, by any chance?'

'Of course not! Why would I do that before I spoke to you?'

'It seems you've done rather a lot already without speaking to me.' Holly's words were clipped and Ryan couldn't fail to get the message that she was upset about this.

Holly was more than upset. She felt like the ground had shifted under her feet—that someone else was taking control of her life. She was being offered something she wanted more than anything, but she couldn't possibly accept. This was cruel, in fact, and a seed of anger blossomed.

'I'm speaking to you now, Holly.' Ryan looked puzzled, which was perfectly understandable. 'I've just been waiting for the right opportunity.' His mouth twisted in a wry smile as he shook his head. 'I'm sorry. I should have known not to go behind your back. I know how fiercely independent you are and how you've managed your illness so far.' He spread his hands in a gesture of surrender. 'There aren't many people who would choose to cope with home dialysis when they live alone. Even fewer people that could manage to keep up such a demanding career. I admire that independence, Holly. It's a big part of why I want to help. And…' the smile tilted up at both corners this time '…I wanted to give you a surprise.'

'You've done that all right.' Ryan's winning smile was impossible not to respond to, but he'd summed up the problem here, hadn't he? Holly managed alone. She made her own decisions and weighed up the consequences of those decisions very carefully beforehand. Some required a lot of thought. Others didn't. Her smile faded.

'You must have realised how impossible it would be for me to accept.'

'Why?'

'You're offering something I wouldn't even ask a blood relative for. You're my boss, Ryan. Way above the level of being equal as a colleague. We're not even…' Holly searched for a word that could demonstrate the gulf between them in a personal field. 'Friends,' she concluded unhappily.

'Aren't we?'

Something in his tone made Holly feel ashamed of what she'd said. As though she was rejecting something of great importance to Ryan. But it was easier from his side of the fence, wasn't it?

'You're my boss, Ryan. You're older and far more experienced than me. You're my teacher. A mentor.' In a position of power that precluded anything as levelling as a personal friendship. 'Our lives don't touch outside working hours.' She sighed, staring down at her tightly linked fingers. 'And I'm a woman, trying to succeed in what is still a male-dominated career path. I'm also trying to cope with a fairly debilitating illness. I resent the limitations it imposes on my life and having to accept help.' She glanced up again. 'That's not to say I'm not enormously grateful for your help. God knows, I'd never have got as far as I have if it hadn't been for you, but you've done enough, Ryan. I couldn't...*wouldn't* accept any more.'

He looked so disappointed, Holly tried to smile.

'Imagine if it didn't work? There I'd be still struggling along and you'd know you'd gone through all that pain, not to mention the risks of having a general anaesthetic, for nothing. I wouldn't be able to work with you any more because I'd feel like such a failure. I'd feel terribly guilty. As though I'd been given a precious gift and I'd just thrown it out or lost it or something. Nobody would blame you for resenting that. It would be way too much of a burden.'

'There's no reason to think it wouldn't work.'

'So there I'd be with a debt of gratitude instead of guilt. It would still be enough to prevent me ever stepping up and working alongside you as an equal.' Holly straightened her back. 'And that's exactly where I intend to be, one day.'

A silence fell, laced with unpleasant hints of how unlikely that scenario was going to be unless Holly *did* get a successful kidney transplant. Holly ignored the vibes. She was really no worse off than she'd been yesterday, was she? And tomorrow was another day. She had learned long ago to take things one day at a time. And maybe...tomorrow, even—that pager on her pocket that linked her to the transplant unit would sound and a well-matched, *anonymous* kidney would be waiting for her.

Ryan nodded slowly, seeming reluctant but resigned to accepting Holly's point of view. But then he smiled. A real Ryan smile, full of warmth and understanding.

'Think about it anyway,' he said softly. 'Please.'

As if she could think about anything else!

Ryan Murphy was the most genuine, caring person Holly had ever met. He couldn't have known how disturbing his offer would be because he would never do anything to deliberately hurt anyone. It hadn't been fair to suggest that their relationship was less meaningful than a friendship because Ryan meant far more than that to Holly.

Far more.

She had the utmost respect for him as a surgeon and the deepest admiration for him as a person. He was, simply, a wonderful man and Holly had wondered on more than one occasion why there wasn't an adoring wife in the picture. As far as she knew, Ryan wasn't in any kind of relationship and that certainly wasn't due to any lack of opportunity. Holly couldn't fail to notice the way women looked at Ryan and she knew exactly what they were thinking. If Holly had been looking for a perfect partner herself, she'd be thinking the same things. Ryan Murphy would have more than fitted any bill of that type.

But she wasn't in a position to *be* looking, was she? And while Ryan's concern and support for her had been so much more than she could have wished for, it had never crossed any professional boundaries. They might think highly of each other but they were colleagues on very dif-

ferent rungs of a professional ladder. Not friends, because
they knew nothing of each other's lives outside work.

Holly wouldn't have a clue what Ryan might be eating
for dinner that night. She put the frozen supermarket dinner
into her microwave with a grimace. This meal was a cop-
out. Only acceptable because the level of protein and
probably anything else in the nutrition stakes was low
enough for the occasional use not to tip her carefully
balanced diet into disarray. Whatever Ryan chose or
possibly cooked for himself, it was bound to be more appealing than the plastic-looking pumpkin and spinach
lasagne she was heating.

He certainly wouldn't be counting out pills to have with
his food either. Working her way methodically along the
row of canisters adorning her window-sill, Holly shook out
the phosphate binders, vitamin and mineral supplements,
the iron tablets and her doses of diuretics and anti-hyper-
tensive medication.

Maybe Ryan had exotic spice jars on his kitchen win-
dowsill. Or herbs growing in pots. Holly wondered what
his kitchen looked like. And his house. She had never
thought about Ryan in such personal terms before and
some of the anger she had felt earlier returned when she
couldn't shake her current train of thought.

Too tired to be hungry, she forced herself to eat and
wondered, in some dismay, whether just voicing that extraordinary offer had been enough to seriously undermine
her professional relationship with the man who headed her
chosen department.

Holly didn't want to have to leave St Margaret's
Children's Hospital. She'd have to go offshore to find
anything similar and with the support team she had in the

renal department of the nearby general hospital, she couldn't afford to look elsewhere. Neither did she want to leave her home town of Auckland, New Zealand. This was her home. Where she wanted to live. And work.

This apartment would never be her ultimate goal, of course, but it was close to both hospitals. It was tiny and low maintenance, and while it might be without soul it was valued nonetheless for its contribution to Holly's independence. Did Ryan have a house rather than an apartment? A cat? A garden, maybe, instead of a sad set of pot-plants on a minuscule balcony? The plants weren't going to receive the attention they urgently needed this evening either. Not when she seemed unable to shake the imaginary comparisons between her life and Ryan's.

That kind of thinking had the potential to destroy things between them. Holly couldn't afford to be envious of anybody and particularly her boss. What if she became resentful that he had a life at all outside work when she didn't? A home and garden to go to? That he had the prospect of that life continuing and including something as wonderful as a family? Something Holly could dream about only if she became healthy again.

Health that could potentially be restored by an offer she couldn't possibly accept.

Why had Ryan made the offer?

Because he felt sorry for her?

Maybe he'd been influenced by recent media coverage of one of New Zealand's foremost sportspeople, Steve Mersey, whose career and Olympic hopes were about to be ended due to the sudden onset of debilitating kidney disease. Complete strangers had started putting up their hands, offering to donate an organ. Had that given Ryan the idea? Did he feel obliged to emulate such altruism because of the type of person he was? Or had he realised how much further it was possible to go in helping someone like her and, having done so much already, felt obliged to go that extra mile?

Either explanation was pretty cringe-making. Holly had done the right thing in refusing to consider acceptance. The only thing she could have done. Now all she needed to do was to stop *thinking* about it, despite Ryan's exhortation.

What she needed, above all, was rest.

And treatment, of course.

With all her essential chores completed, Holly moved to her bedroom, a small room in which the bed was actually the least significant piece of furniture. Tonight it seemed far more depressing than usual to retire to a room that would not have looked out of place attached to some hospital ward.

Her dialysis machine was the size of an average refrigerator. It would have been enough to make the room look clinical all by itself, but it was far from alone. The large water purifier was flanked by a tall cabinet that held ranks of huge bottles filled with the fluid needed for the machine. A chest of drawers beside that held saline and tubing lines. A trolley with slide-out trays housed alcohol wipes, needles, tapes, dressings and all the other paraphernalia that went along with home dialysis.

The routine of setting up was automatic. Inserting the two needles into the surgically enlarged vein on her forearm was virtually painless. Now all Holly needed to do was wait. In a matter of four to six hours, the entire volume of blood in her body would have passed through the dialysis machine at least six times, having waste products and excess fluid drawn out.

Holly often used most of this time to sit, propped up by pillows, in her bed, studying or catching up on journals. She had brought home a textbook she wanted to read, detailing the latest techniques in arterial-switch procedures such as baby Grace would need to undergo shortly, but she simply couldn't find the energy or enthusiasm to open it.

On top of a physically challenging day, Ryan's offer had left her utterly drained and Holly would have to sleep while the machine did its life-prolonging magic tonight. It also seemed the only way she could turn off the endless treadmill of the thoughts that interview with Ryan had sparked. Tomorrow she would feel so much better she'd be able to carry on as normal. And, with a bit of luck, Ryan's offer wouldn't change anything other than her appreciation of what a kind person he was.

The call to the intensive care unit came as Holly stepped through the front doors of St Margaret's at 8 a.m. the following day. Rather than waste time by finding a phone to contact the unit staff, Holly just kept going. It was so good to be able to move along the still quiet corridors and feel as if she was walking normally and not pushing her body through air that felt as thick as treacle. At this rate she would be actually in the unit by the time she would have completed a phone call.

The speed of Holly's response had far more to do with her renewed level of energy than the early morning absence of obstacles caused by people or equipment, and she took full advantage of the physical strength, bypassing any wait for a lift and heading for the stairs.

It had to be Callum that was causing concern in the unit and the page had been urgent. Hearing footsteps far more rapid than her own behind her on the stairs was frustrating. Dialysis might be magic but it couldn't work a miracle, like giving her the sudden ability to race up stairs two at a time as someone else was obviously doing.

'Holly!' The steps slowed to match hers and Ryan's smile was delighted. 'You must be feeling a lot better to be using the stairs. That's great!'

Holly just nodded, not wanting Ryan to know that climbing stairs half as quickly as him had left her somewhat breathless. He held the door open as they reached the second floor.

'You've been paged by ICU?'

She nodded again.

'Any idea what's going on?'

'We'll soon find out.' Holly's words were clipped but not just by lack of breath. She was fighting a dread that her first VSD repair might be going pear-shaped. Had her stitches not been quite deep enough or sufficiently close together? Was Callum bleeding around his heart and suffering a life-threatening tamponade? Respiratory failure or a hypertensive crisis? Had he spiked a fever or developed renal failure?

Ryan touched her arm as they reached the unit. 'Don't worry so much,' he said. 'Whatever it is, we'll sort it out. Together.'

Ryan's reassurance, even his presence, was kind of like dialysis for her soul, Holly thought wryly. Fears and insecurities got filtered out and confidence renewed. She could focus and perform and not be intimidated when pushed to voice her own opinions.

Such as what she thought about the concern raised by Callum's heart rate and rhythm. Disturbances were frequent following open heart surgery and fortunately the abnormal pattern being recorded on Callum's ECG was not immediately life-threatening.

'It's supraventricular,' Holly said in response to Ryan's raised eyebrows. 'The drop in blood pressure is most probably rate-related.'

'How do you want to manage it?'

'I'll consult with Cardiology,' Holly decided. 'It's A-fib so adenosine is probably the drug of choice. If it continues, a digoxin infusion should give us sinus rhythm again or drop the ventricular rate, but that's much slower. If neither works, we'd need to look at other anti-arrhythmic agents or a DC conversion.'

A telephone call to one of the cardiology consultants led to a rapid instigation of treatment, but by the time Callum was showing a good response and his anxious parents had been soothed, Ryan and Holly were running late for their 9 a.m. theatre start time.

'Slow down,' Ryan complained as they made their way to the changing rooms adjacent to the operating theatre suite. 'I'm not as young as I used to be.'

'Neither am I.' Holly threw a quick grin over her shoulder. 'I turned thirty last week, you know.'

'No, I didn't know.' Ryan quickened his pace to walk alongside her. 'Hey, happy birthday—belatedly.'

'Thanks.'

'Was it a good party?'

'I didn't have a party,' Holly said quickly. She certainly didn't want to add to any unfortunate impression she might have given yesterday that she didn't like Ryan enough to consider him a friend and therefore he hadn't been invited to any party she had held. 'I didn't really feel like celebrating my slide into middle age.'

Ryan snorted. 'I'm thirty-six,' he said indignantly, 'and I don't consider myself anywhere near middle-aged, thank you.' He pushed open the door leading to the male side of the changing-room complex then paused. 'Don't you like parties?' he asked curiously.

'I like other people's parties,' Holly told him lightly. 'Not mine.' She grinned again. 'That way, I don't have to clean up the mess.'

Inside the changing room, Holly's face stilled as she sighed. Why had she started that conversation in the first place? Reaching her fourth decade should have been worth celebrating. The trouble was, in her case she wasn't just marking a significant milestone in the passage of time. It would have been more a celebration that her time hadn't run out.

Yet.

Why hadn't Holly wanted a party to celebrate such an important birthday?

She should have had candles and a cake and people around to let her know how special the day was. How special *she* was. Ryan wished *he* had known. He could have given her a hug even, without stepping over the boundaries he observed so carefully. He should have known, dammit. He must have seen or signed papers that had to have had the date on them often enough. Perhaps he was closer to being middle-aged than he suspected and was developing a selective memory.

Pulling on white rubber theatre boots, Ryan moved to the dispensing box on the wall of the changing room to pull out the disposable bootees to cover the boots' soles. Then he plucked a hat and mask from adjoining boxes.

He *was* feeling older today. Older and wiser.

He'd gone about it all the wrong way and he'd tried so hard to do things just right, too. To keep it all on a kind of professional basis so that Holly would not be influenced by how strongly he felt about it all. Maybe he had tried *too* hard. He'd done such a good job of not taking advantage of his position of power and acting on any personal interest in Holly that she didn't even consider him to be a friend.

That had hurt.

A lot.

Ryan's attention to scrubbing his hands in preparation for surgery was always thorough but it was more vigorous than usual this morning after his registrar joined him at the basins. He welcomed the sting of the bristles on the tender flesh between the base of his fingers.

It was just as well Holly had no idea of the real reason for him making the offer of donating a kidney.

That he was in love with her. That part of his soul was sharing her physical deterioration and would, if she died, be lost for ever.

Boy, would that scare her off in a hurry! She didn't want to be burdened by gratitude or guilt on a purely professional level. Imagine if she knew how he felt and took it the wrong way—thinking he might be trying to pull her into a closer relationship by offering such a valuable gift?

She would be appalled. Hell, she didn't even consider him to be a *friend*.

But how could she not be aware of a bond that went so far past the normal interaction of a registrar and consultant? Had he been so good at hiding the gradual development of his feelings that Holly, and any onlookers, assumed they simply shared a passion for their work that made them inseparable during working hours?

It was entirely possible, Ryan realised as their case for the morning got under way. Their twelve-year-old male patient had had a congenital lesion of aortic stenosis treated by a balloon valvuloplasty in infancy but residual stenosis and incompetence had led to an increasingly severe degree of symptoms which meant it was no longer advisable to wait until growth had completely stopped before replacing the valve. Besides, young Daniel was also very keen to play rugby and strenuous activity had so far been denied him because of the risk of sudden death. If all went well with the new valve he was going to receive today, his life would change considerably for the better.

It was a technically challenging procedure due to the congenital malformation of the valve but Ryan was more than happy to keep up a running commentary and answer Holly's eager queries.

'We make the transverse aortotomy about fifteen millimetres above the level of the right coronary artery. We don't want to be any lower because that can jeopardise the artery and create problems in seating the valve.'

'What happens if you go higher?'

'Not much. It's easy to angle down and any lip can be retracted.'

That was typical of Holly. She had always demonstrated the ability to determine all possible alternatives to any course of action and weigh up the potential consequences. She was sharp enough to do it almost instantly and it was a skill that would stand her in very good stead when she got to be a consultant surgeon herself.

If she got to be a consultant surgeon.

Given a technical problem, Ryan was confident that Holly could make a correct choice of an appropriate course of action. He spared a very fleeting moment of concentration to wonder why she couldn't apply the same skill to a personal arena.

Maybe she would. Maybe Holly just needed some time to get used to the idea and if he didn't push her she would be able to view it as an independent choice and find a way to get past what she saw as unacceptable potential consequences.

All he could do was wait. And hope. And help her to do what she wanted to do with her life as far as he was able or allowed to help.

'You did such a good job on that patch yesterday, Holly,' he said, when the more technical aspects of preparation had been completed. 'How about tackling part of this prosthetic valve insertion?'

She *was* feeling a lot better today. The sparkle Ryan detected in the dark eyes that flashed up to meet his held no hint of any doubt in her own ability. Or any desire not to be given that level of responsibility. Holly was eager to spread her wings again and Ryan only too happy to support her.

As he always would be, given the chance.

Never mind anything *too* personal. As Ryan guided Holly through what was a new procedure for her, he was very aware of how much less satisfying his job would be without Holly to share his fascination in operating on what was, for them both, at the top of the list of the vital organs humans possessed.

There had to be a way to secure a future for Holly because Ryan didn't want to even consider the alternative.

And he wouldn't. Not yet.

CHAPTER THREE

'MICHAELA! Hello, sweetheart!'

Holly's intended destination, to visit Daniel who was back in the ward only three days after his aortic valve replacement, simply had to be postponed. Michaela Brown had never been one of Holly's patients but the tiny thirteen-year-old was a favourite and sadly one of the most frequent inpatients in the cardiology ward.

There was an empty chair beside the one Michaela was using in the central corridor. Holly sat down on it.

'What are you doing here?'

'I had...to come back in.' The blue tinge to the girl's lips was obvious despite the nasal cannula leading to the portable oxygen cylinder on the floor beside her chair. 'My kidneys aren't...working so well.'

'Oh.' Holly's face scrunched into lines of sympathy. Michaela's heart failure had been getting less and less responsive to the raft of medication she was on. Renal failure could be a sign that they were getting near the end of the road but Holly had to squash her dismay before that could show on her face so she smiled instead. 'That's no good, hon. But what I meant was, why are you sitting all by yourself in the corridor?'

Michaela was never alone. At least one of her parents was always close by and her twin five-year-old sisters were devoted little shadows whenever possible. It had been the bond between the small, identical versions of Michaela and their big sister that had first attracted Holly's attention a year ago but it hadn't taken long to understand why this girl was the sun that the whole family orbited.

Huge blue eyes beneath a mop of golden curls gleamed with sheer joy in response to Holly's query. It didn't seem to matter that every breath was a struggle to provide oxygen to the inadequate level of circulation her failing heart could provide.

'The twins are…making a surprise. I'm not…allowed to see.' Michaela took several quick breaths and then lowered her voice. 'I think it's…a picnic…on my bed.'

Holly stood up and peeped through the small square window in the door to the nearest single room. Sure enough, two small girls were arranging paper plates holding bite-sized treats like fairy bread and grapes. Their mother, Robyn, was pouring soft drink into plastic cups.

'Is it…a picnic?'

'Not telling.' Holly grinned and sat down again. 'How's school going?'

'Good. I miss heaps, though.'

'You're more than smart enough to catch up. How's Toby?'

'He's good, too. But I'm not riding…just now.'

Of course she wasn't. Michaela had been a star junior rider in the pony club until a year ago. The rare complication of an ordinary viral illness had given her congestive cardiomyopathy—a dilated, floppy left ventricle incapable of pumping blood effectively.

Michaela had not come under Ryan's surgical firm's care because the only surgery that could help was a heart transplant. The cardiology team was doing its best to keep her alive in the hope of that happening, but the chance that Michaela could ever ride her beloved pony, Toby, again was slim at best.

Her pets had always been a favourite topic of conversation, however.

'Does Toby still like eating jelly snakes?'

'Yeah… I've got a…new kitten now.'

'Oh, cute! What colour?'

'Black.'

'Girl or boy?'

'Girl.'

'What's her name?'

'Sooty.' Michaela looked disgusted. 'The twins…named it before they…gave her to me.' Her face lit up again as a man approached. 'Hi, Daddy!'

'Hey, gorgeous.' Michaela's father was carrying a wicker basket with flaps, and Holly was as curious as the girl beside her. Wasn't the picnic food already in Michaela's room?

'What's…in the basket?'

'Not telling.' Don Brown looked stern. 'It's supposed to be a surprise.'

The faint mewing sound that followed his words led to a startled silence.

Michaela giggled. 'You're…busted, Dad.'

Don cast an anxious glance at Holly. 'I'm breaking the rules, aren't I?'

Holly stood up. 'I didn't hear a thing,' she claimed. She winked at Michaela. 'See you later. I hope you enjoy your lunch.'

* * *

Daniel's lunchtime food and entertainment was a lot less inventive but the atmosphere around him was happy without the poignancy of Michaela's case. His mother was pinning up pictures of Daniel's heroes, the members of his favourite Auckland rugby team who were also part of the national All Blacks squad.

Sitting on the end of his bed, discussing the finer moments of the last match they had played, was Ryan.

'And did you see that drop kick? Scott Grigg's the man, isn't he?'

'He's called Sox.'

'Why?' Holly hadn't heard the popular rugby player's nickname. 'Because he has stinky feet?'

'Please!' Ryan's look was as pitying as Daniel's. 'We're discussing the man of the match here.'

'D'you know he's only eighteen?' Daniel twisted in bed to look up at the poster in prime position. 'And he didn't even start playing rugby until he was thirteen.' He looked back at Ryan. 'I'll be able to start playing soon, won't I?'

'At the rate you're recovering, it won't be too long before you can get active, but we need to keep a good eye on you for a while yet.'

'Will I get out of hospital in time to go to the next game? It's in Auckland. I was too sick to go last time they played here.'

'We'll see what we can do,' Ryan promised, before excusing himself. Outside Daniel's room, he raised an eyebrow in Holly's direction. 'How are things in the unit?'

'Grace is still running a bit of a temperature. Her white count is normal but there's the possibility it's some kind of infection. The medical team isn't happy to clear her for surgery until they have more idea of what might be going on. Leo's clear for surgery if you want to swap their slots tomorrow.'

Ryan nodded. 'Let's go and have a chat to his parents.'

They passed Michaela's door and Ryan's casual sideways glance made him come to an abrupt halt. Holly stifled a giggle but the sound earned her a suspicious glance.

'You know what's going on in there, don't you?'

She tried to look convincingly innocent. 'Michaela's back in. Sounds like things are deteriorating, unfortunately. She said something about her kidneys not functioning too well and…'

But Ryan didn't appear to be listening. He grabbed Holly's elbow and tugged it to pull her closer. It wasn't until Holly co-operated, turned and spotted who was at the end of the corridor that she realised what Ryan was doing. The hospital's CEO's personal assistant, a woman not noted for her sense of humour, was making visit to the ward. If she saw the additional visitor in Michaela's room, the family picnic was unlikely to end on a very good note.

Both Ryan and Holly were quite tall enough to block any inadvertent view through the window in the closed door behind them.

'What's the creatinine level?' Ryan then queried with uncharacteristic brusqueness.

Holly blinked. 'Um…'

'You'd better get on top of this, Holly.' Ryan was frowning. 'Deterioration in renal function is going to mean having to juggle anti-failure medication. Really, I'm surprised at you for not having the lab results available already.'

The tone, suggestive of a professional rebuke, earned Holly a similar frown from the passing administrator, but the woman clearly wasn't going to interrupt such an exchange. Ryan waited until she was turning into the nurse manager's office and then he smiled apologetically, turning to wave through the window.

'Maybe you should suggest that the four-footed friend goes back in its box before the white witch returns.' The remnants of his smile faded as he turned back to Holly. 'The clock's ticking a bit loudly in there, isn't it?' His face was sombre now. 'I've got a quick phone call I really have to make, Holly. Meet you in Leo's room in ten minutes?'

'Sure.'

Ryan had turned away quickly enough for Holly not to have picked up anything personal in his glance, but it surfaced anyway as she let herself into Michaela's room to join the picnic for a minute or two.

Not that Ryan had said anything more about his offer, but it was impossible not to feel a personal connection with someone else on a waiting list for a transplant. Holly received a hug from the twins and smiles from Michaela's parents as she sat on the end of the bed to admire Sooty properly.

If only it was something as simple as a kidney that Michaela needed so desperately. The teenager was loved by more than her immediate family. Aunts, uncles, cousins—even grandparents—would be queuing up to be tested if they had the opportunity to do anything to save her.

The warning about Sooty needing to keep a lower profile resulted in one of the twins stuffing the kitten beneath the covers of Michaela's bed and the very mobile lump provoked complete hilarity. Holly was still smiling as she left the room a short time later but, like Ryan, the smile faded rapidly as the reality of the situation hit home.

Anyone who knew Michaela would be touched by her plight. The girl's courage, humour and ability to find joy in life despite everything was inspirational. The sudden notion that if it *had* been a kidney Michaela needed and she'd had no close relatives and Holly had been healthy, *she* would seriously have considered getting herself tested as a match was something of a revelation.

Had *that* been why Ryan had made his offer?

Not that it made any difference to her being in a position to accept, but the thought did give Holly an odd buzz. She had only ever been doing what she had to do in order to survive, but she had tried to do it without losing her sense of humour or appreciation of what life still had to offer. She had never set out to impress others but something about the idea that she might have touched Ryan in the same way Michaela's case touched her made Holly feel a kind of shy pride in the way she had coped so far.

And somehow it made persevering just that much more worthwhile. Holly could even face the new prospect of dialysis every second night with renewed determination. It was ironic that Ryan had used a measure of renal function for the pretence of a professional conversation to cover their blocking of Michaela's window. Holly had just had her own results back that morning and things were not looking great. Thank goodness tomorrow was the last day of a working week that was proving unusually stressful.

Sooty the kitten had provided a lift in what would have otherwise been a depressing occasion with yet another admission and a serious complication for Michaela Brown.

Another lift came towards the end of the day. The arrival of three members of Auckland's Blues Super 12 rugby team would have caused a stir anywhere. That they were being followed by a television news crew made everyone stop and stare.

'We've come to visit Daniel,' Scott Griggs informed the charge nurse.

'We hear he's a bit of a fan of ours and he's just been through some major surgery,' his companion added. 'We've got a ball for him.'

Not just any ball. This one had been signed by every member of the Blues. It was a treasure.

Holly dropped the last set of case notes she'd been returning back into their slot in the trolley and pushed it clear of the entourage. So they'd heard Daniel was a rugby fan? And 'Sox' was actually there to present the treasure? There was only one person who could have arranged that, and Holly went searching.

She found Ryan in his office.

'So that was what the phone call was about? How on earth did you work that?'

'Friend of a friend.' Ryan grinned. 'I was in the first fifteen at school, you know. Some of my mates went on to bigger and better things in rugby.'

Holly stared at him in amazement. With his impressive height of well over six feet and a solid build, she could imagine him being able to provide muscle to any scrum. But, of course, she hadn't known that. She didn't really know anything about the man Ryan was. She only knew the surgeon. A medical professional who would go out of his way twice in one day to make life a little better for the children he came into contact with. Holly had to swallow hard in order to clear the painful constriction in her throat.

'Has anyone ever told you what a nice person you are, Ryan Murphy?'

He shrugged off the compliment. 'So Sox is there himself?' He sounded thoughtful as he stood up. 'I might just wander across and say hello.' His smile had an appealing element of embarrassment at any obvious eagerness he'd displayed. He made an effort to sound more casual. 'Want to come?'

Holly shook her head. 'I reckon it's more of a boy thing. You go.' Her smile was mischievous. 'You never know your luck—you might get an autograph.'

'Won't be long,' Ryan promised. 'We need to duck into ICU and review Grace before we clock out. Wait for me?'

'Sure.'

Holly was grateful for a few minutes' respite. The excitement in the ward was more than she could have handled with the crippling weariness taking hold again. She felt a wave of nausea and sank into Ryan's chair as soon as he'd left the office. The screen on his computer provided a distraction. Her boss had clearly been using a few spare minutes to catch up on current affairs and the headline stories of the day from one of the major newspapers were on display. One of them caught Holly's eye immediately.

BACKLASH FROM TRANSPLANT HOPEFULS

She clicked on the headline and brought up the story. A group of people on the national waiting list for organ transplants were outraged by the response to the publicity given to Steve Mersey's medical crisis. If people were so keen to donate an organ to a complete stranger, the group queried, why didn't they make themselves available to one of the hundreds of hopefuls who were waiting years for the chance of a cadaveric transplant? Why did being good at a sporting endeavour make someone so much more deserving? Maybe these people should log onto one of the websites devoted to people trying to find a match and help an ordinary person to continue living, they argued.

Holly was on the national waiting list. She was probably facing a longer wait than most to find a perfect match, but she couldn't agree with the outrage. Offering an organ was an heroic thing to do. You'd have to be touched very deeply to consider making that offer. The way Holly was by Michaela, for instance. The way people out there were touched by the story of a national sporting hero. But to make such an offer to a complete stranger? No way.

And yet, wasn't Holly demanding a stranger's kidney for herself in preference to one from someone who knew her and was possibly touched by her own case? Was she guilty of a double standard here?

The end of the article listed web links for anyone interested in learning more about the need for organ transplants. Almost idly, still seeking a distraction from the physical symptoms resulting from exhaustion, Holly clicked on one, and an organ-match site came up instantly. It was easy to click on 'kidneys' and then 'patient profiles'. Holly scrolled down to find page after page of links to people begging for help. Subject lines like:

Help. I need a kidney to live
Single mum needs kidney
Please—read my story—I'm desperate!
Are you the one?

It was all a bit painfully close to home but delving more deeply was irresistible. Why hadn't she ever been tempted to join any support groups or tried to make contact with other people in her position? Independence could be a lonely business.

The website was based in the United States and Holly

clicked on one of the profile titles to learn more. The single mother's name was Marci and she was only twenty-three. She had done dialysis every day of her pregnancy and the father of her baby had walked out when her son had been two months old. Her baby was now approaching his first birthday and Marci was begging for a chance to watch him grow. She needed a donor who was O or A positive and under 'requirements of donor' she simply asked for anyone with a giving heart.

Ryan Murphy had a 'giving heart'. Maybe Marci would be lucky enough to meet someone like him.

A thirty-year-old male called Mike was advertising for a donor with B or O type blood. He wanted to be able to sleep without a noisy machine keeping him awake. He wanted a chance to have a relationship but the only girl he'd ever brought home had been freaked out by the machinery.

Holly could identify with that. Her machinery had been enough to end a relationship she'd had great hopes for once. Mike was the same age as her. He hadn't given up hope of finding someone yet. He just wanted to be healthy enough to try. In his requirements for a donor, he asked for the chance to get to know the person who would be giving such a gift and for them to get to know him.

One patient profile had been deleted. Instead there was a message from the father of the kidney-disease sufferer saying that a kidney was no longer needed because, sadly, his daughter had died on the fifteenth of July. He expressed heartfelt thanks to all those who had responded and tried to help. But then she found another, full of the joy of success. There was even a video clip to watch with an interview from the patient, a woman, and the donor—a friend of her husband's. He was a part of their family now and they were all working together to set up a trust that could help others. The donor urged others to follow his example, claiming that he had never done anything so worthwhile in his entire life.

A fifty-eight-year-old woman, Gloria, pleaded for help. She suffered from diabetes, was blind, had high blood pressure and cardiac problems and had had triple bypass surgery a year ago. She'd had countless operations but her venous access kept failing with clots or infections and she was now trying to cope with peritoneal dialysis. Time that she desperately wanted to spend with her seven grandchildren was running out and she was now too weak to leave her house.

Almost unconsciously, Holly stroked her forearm. Her current fistula, where an artery and vein were joined to make the access point larger, was working fine, but it was her second site. Her other forearm was scarred and lumpy where the first had failed. She was otherwise quite healthy, though. What hope did this poor woman have? People would read her story and be quite justified in thinking that giving a healthy kidney to someone with so many other problems would be a waste.

Holly read on. And on. She wished Ryan would come back and distract her because she couldn't stop reading all these sad pleas for help. So many people with so many different lives, but they all wanted the same thing. Some were her own age but others, like Gloria, were much older and they still weren't prepared to give up. Some wanted a chance to continue their careers, others just wanted more time with the people they loved. There was something touching in every story.

How thrilled would any one of these people be to have

someone like Ryan in their lives, offering what they wanted most? None of them would turn him down.

So what the hell did Holly think she was doing?

What would happen next year, maybe, or the year after, when she still hadn't been lucky enough to find a transplant match and she was too sick to continue working at all or even live independently? Would she be living with the regret of not accepting Ryan's offer?

Would he go to her funeral and feel sad or possibly angry that things could have been very different?

Holly was really fighting tears now. She didn't want to die. She wanted what all these people wanted.

A chance to live. To live a normal life. To work and play. To love and be loved.

Ryan strode back towards his office with a spring in his step and a smile on his face that wouldn't go away.

He'd never seen a kid as happy as Daniel had been. That rugby ball wouldn't be leaving his hands for a very long time. He'd probably sleep with a huge lump under his pillow. Being interviewed for television had been exciting, but it had come a poor second to the opportunity to actually meet his rugby heroes. Poor kid had been completely tongue-tied for the first ten minutes of the visit.

Hopefully, Holly was still waiting for him. He hadn't intended to be so long, but the television crew had wanted some detail on the type of surgery Daniel had been through, and good publicity for the hospital never went astray when it came to fundraising time.

Which reminded him, he needed to think about getting sponsorship for the annual City to Surf fun run, which was less than three months away. St Margaret's staff and supporters got dressed up in sometimes ridiculous costumes and went out to demonstrate how unfit most of them were, but last year they had raised enough money to purchase a new state-of-the-art incubator for the neonatal intensive care unit so the cause was very worthwhile.

Ryan was toying with various ideas for costumes that wouldn't prove too embarrassing but would still be entertaining enough to elicit generous donations from the public *en route*, and was still smiling as he basked in the aftermath of sharing young Daniel's happiness when he opened his office door.

Never had a smile been wiped off his face so fast.

Holly was *crying*!

Ryan crossed the space between them in less than two strides.

'My God, Holly, what's happened? Are you all right?'

'I'm fine.' Holly blinked furiously and scrubbed at her face, but another tear escaped. 'I'm fine, really.'

'Oh, right.' Ryan held out his hand. 'Come here, Holly.'

She let him pull her to her feet and then he kept pulling until she was in his arms and then, for the first time ever, he hugged his registrar.

'You can't tell me it's nothing,' he murmured. 'Not when I've never seen you cry before.'

She made a sound halfway between a hiccup and a laugh but she didn't try to pull away. And it was *so* good to feel his arms around her like this.

Too good.

Ryan eased his hold and Holly stepped back instantly. The tears had vanished.

'Sorry,' she said. 'But you only have yourself to blame.'

'What have *I* done?'

'You've been gone so long. I was amusing myself on the net. I started reading about the flak that Steve Mersey has generated with publicity on his kidney problems but I ended up reading about a whole bunch of people trying to find a new kidney. Some of the stories were so sad.'

'Oh…' Ryan wasn't sure what to say. Holly hadn't shown any signs of wanting to revisit their conversation of a few days ago and he was determined not to put any pressure on her, but she was upset right now and he had to try and help. 'Do you want to talk about it?'

'Have we got time? Shouldn't we be going to see Grace?'

'Grace isn't going anywhere. And neither are we, until we've had a chance to talk. Anything that's made you cry has got to be important.'

Holly sank slowly back into Ryan's chair behind his desk. She glanced at the computer screen for a long, silent moment and then turned her gaze up to Ryan.

'This…' she waved her hand at the website still showing on the screen '…has made me really think about the people who offer a kidney to others.' She took a deep breath and let it out in a sigh. 'I can understand why people do it for a family member or their partners. I can even sympathise with the people who've read about Steve Mersey and come forward because he's famous and people are touched by his success, but…'

Ryan was way ahead of her. Holly wanted to know what it was about *her* that was special to him. And if he started telling her that, he might reveal far too much and put Holly off completely. He had to think fast. And carefully. Ryan was hopeless at lying but he didn't have to tell the *whole* truth, did he?

He sat on the edge of his desk, the movement distracting Holly from trying to finish her sentence. He kept his gaze on her face and was pleased that his smile seemed to chase away some of the tension darkening her eyes.

'This isn't the first time I've done something like this, Holly.'

Her eyebrows rose sharply. 'Just how many kidneys do you have, Ryan Murphy?'

He laughed. So did Holly and suddenly the tension seemed to evaporate.

'The last time was a donation for a bone-marrow transplant.'

Holly looked interested rather than surprised. 'Was it successful?'

'No.'

'Oh…that must have been awful.'

Ryan merely gave a brief nod. It was Holly he wanted to talk about, not himself. 'It wasn't a perfect match and it wasn't enough to combat the disease. Nothing like the same scenario as giving you a kidney. I had a general anaesthetic for the marrow harvest so I took pretty much the same risk. A minimal risk, as far as I'm concerned,' he added firmly.

'You'd have to live with a single kidney for the rest of your life. That's a risk as well.'

'Also minimal. One kidney is perfectly adequate and I'm not intending to take up playing rugby again or engage in any other activities that might risk injury to a single organ.' He frowned at Holly. 'I hope you're not planning to take up paragliding or rock climbing or something.'

She grinned but was still intent on her own line of thought.

'What does your family think about you giving bits of yourself away?'

'I don't have any close family. Or any dependants.'

'But you might well get married one day. Your wife might not appreciate some other woman running around with one of her husband's kidneys.'

It was Ryan's turn to take a deep, and hopefully settling, breath. He couldn't say what sprang to mind—that the only woman he could conceive of wanting to spend the rest of his life with would be the one that *had* that kidney.

'If I ever got married again,' he said carefully, 'it would be to someone who was special enough to understand and appreciate why I had done something like that.'

Holly's jaw had dropped. '*Again*?'

'My wife—Elise—was the person I donated bone marrow to.'

He could see the wheels turning. Could see Holly trying to refocus some mental picture. Trying to imagine his wife, perhaps? Wondering if she reminded him of Elise strongly enough to have prompted his offer? He couldn't let her think that and it was just so far from the truth it should be easy to refute.

'I nearly became a vet,' he told Holly. She blinked at the apparently random comment but Ryan carried on. 'I had a dog when I was a kid. Flint. A big, fat, black Labrador. We grew up together. By the time I was fifteen, Flint was old. He had arthritis and must have been in a lot of pain a lot of the time, but he never complained. He took what life dished out and he made the best of it. Even when he was too old and sore to chase a stick he was still a happy dog and he was so good to have around. I think his attitude to life helped me through more than one teenage crisis.'

Holly was listening but her frown of concentration suggested she was still perplexed.

'I went into medicine and paediatrics in particular because I see a lot of that kind of "Flint philosophy" in kids. They can face the most appalling medical conditions or a limited life span and still get on with life and give and receive so much happiness. And then you have perfectly healthy people out there who can always find something to moan about. They could learn a hell of a lot from those kids. *I* find it inspiring every day.'

Holly was nodding now. Was she thinking about Michaela, perhaps? Or Daniel or Leo or any one of the dozens of children's lives they had been involved with?

'I married Elise when I was still in med school,' Ryan continued quietly. 'More than ten years ago. She got diagnosed with non-Hodgkin's lymphoma a year later and I think she gave up on the day she got diagnosed. There's a seventy-five per cent chance of long-term survival with non-Hodgkin's patients now, but Elise refused to try a second round of chemo. She gave up trying to live and became a permanent invalid. She only went through the bone-marrow transplant because I was so determined, but it wasn't enough. She died six months later.'

Holly's soft words broke the silence that fell. 'I'm so sorry, Ryan.'

'It happened,' Ryan said evenly. 'It was a long time ago and it was part of what life dished out. Maybe that's what drew me to working with kids in the first place. They have so much of that Flint philosophy. So do you, Holly. In spades.'

This was great. He was comparing her to his dog instead of his wife but at least Holly was looking thoughtful rather than offended.

'I admire your courage,' he added. 'And the way you don't let your illness hold you back from what you give to your patients and their families. You touch a lot of lives, Holly. You help so many people. I'd like to be able to look back on my life and know that I did something special to help *you*.'

He could see the instant the tears welled up in Holly's eyes because he held her gaze so intently. She blinked and tiny droplets caught in the dark tangle of her lashes. Then a single tear rolled down the side of her nose.

'So…' Holly cleared her throat but her words were still choked. 'Your offer is still open, then?'

'Of course it is.' Ryan couldn't stop himself reaching out and gently running his thumb down the side of her nose to collect that tear.

'In that case…' Holly's gaze slid sideways for a long moment, seemingly focussed on the computer screen. Then it came back to catch and hold Ryan's.

He could see the kind of determination he'd come to associate with Holly Williams in that gaze. Fear and hope in equal quantities that somehow came together to create that amazing courage she possessed.

She cleared her throat again. 'I'd like to accept your offer, please, Ryan. As long as we *are* as compatible as you think.'

'We're compatible, Holly. You'll be convinced as soon as Doug shows you what a perfect match we are.' Ryan couldn't stop smiling. He was about to put himself through a probably painful and unpleasant procedure and he'd never felt so ridiculously pleased about anything. And Holly was smiling back at him.

'Perfect match, huh?'

'Perfect,' Ryan said with assurance. 'You just wait and see.'

CHAPTER FOUR

RENAL physician Doug Smiley was more than living up to his name.

He was beaming, in fact, as he looked at the two people sitting opposite his desk.

'This is great! Fabulous news! You've made *my* day so you must be absolutely thrilled, Holly.'

Holly nodded but an anxious frown creased her brow. 'I just hope it's going to work, Doug—for Ryan's sake as much as mine. I'd hate him to go through with all this for nothing.'

Doug waved a hand dismissively. 'No reason to think negatively. You two couldn't be a better match as far as the preliminary testing went. We'll have to run a repeat series to recheck antibodies and cross-matching, of course. And you'll need a few extras this time, Ryan, like hepatitis and AIDS screening.'

Ryan didn't seem to share Holly's embarrassment at any oblique reference to his sex life. He merely nodded.

'I'm confident they'll all come back with no nasty surprises.'

'So am I.' Doug nodded agreement, smiling at Holly again. Pushing sixty now, Holly's renal physician was clearly very fond of his patient. 'And the transplant team will want a fairly in-depth look at your family history for things like cancer, diabetes, hypertension and so on.'

'That might be a bit trickier,' Ryan said. 'I'm an only child and my parents both died in their fifties in a bus crash when they were touring Europe on a second honeymoon.'

'Grandparents?'

'All got to their eighties in pretty good health. And I've still got my paternal grandfather around. Pop's ninety-six and he can still beat me at chess.'

'Fabulous!'

Holly was silent as the two men conversed but her head was spinning. She had just learned more about Ryan in thirty seconds than she had ever known. Somehow it didn't surprise her that he would take the time to play what could be a lengthy game with an ancient relative but she was surprised to learn he was an orphan and that he played chess at all.

She joined in the chuckle when Doug made a comment about it being nice to have a kidney that was coming from a good home, but as she left the office with Ryan a few minutes later Holly was starting to wonder how much more she was going to learn about Ryan before all this was over.

Possibly a lot more than she'd bargained for.

'Let's duck into the treatment room in the ward,' Ryan suggested. 'We can take each other's bloods off and get a head start on those tests. That way the results will all be there before we meet the transplant team in the next day or two.'

There was nothing unusual in Ryan taking a blood sample from Holly. He had often drawn blood for her routine monthly antibodies check and anything else Doug might have ordered simply to save her the trouble of finding a venipuncturist during their already overly busy days.

Somehow, it felt different this time. Holly sat on the

edge of the bed in the treatment room and pushed her sleeve up, and was suddenly embarrassed by the lumpy scar of the old fistula. Ryan tightened the tourniquet around her upper arm and Holly didn't need to be told to open and close her fist a few times.

Maybe it felt different today because the tests were for such a different purpose. Or maybe it was because she was suddenly connected to Ryan in a far more personal way. It was all happening so quickly it was no wonder she hadn't quite got her head around it all yet.

Whatever was causing it, Holly was acutely aware of Ryan's touch. It was as gentle as it always was as he felt for a vein and swabbed her skin but she could feel it much more intensely. Something strange had been sensitised and it was disturbing.

Even more disturbing was having to return the favour for him. She saw him in theatre scrubs several times a week, so why did rolling up the sleeve of his dress shirt make it seem like more of his skin was exposed than she had ever seen before? And why hadn't she ever noticed that the tawny hair on his tanned skin was an exact match for the streaks in the hair on his head?

'Veins like drainpipes,' she quipped, in an effort to distract herself, as she clicked the tourniquet closed. 'Can't miss, can I?'

'Hope not.' Ryan smiled. 'Unless you're after revenge for the number of times I've stuck a needle into you.'

'I don't think so.' Holly bounced a vein lightly with her fingertips and then reached for an alcohol wipe. Its cool dampness was welcome. How weird was it to be touching Ryan like this? No wonder she was getting this odd tingle that appeared to connect her fingertips to her spine.

She held the needle in his vein as steady as possible as she pushed the rubber ends of the vacuum tubes onto the connecting end of the needle. Blood pulsed into tube after tube.

'You might need a cup of tea and a sandwich after this.'

'Doubt it. I lose far more every time I donate blood.'

Another surprise. 'Are you a regular blood donor, then?'

'I've always felt obliged to, what with having one of the rarer groups. They're always short and patients can run into real trouble if they can't get a match. Knowing how much can get used with cardiac patients started me off, I guess.'

'Maybe you've got a thing about giving bits of yourself away.' Holly pulled the needle free quickly and pressed a swab to the puncture site. 'You're a generous man, Ryan.'

He grunted in an unimpressed fashion, taking over putting pressure on the swab.

'And you play *chess*.'

'Is that so strange?'

Holly busied herself tipping the glass tubes to mix the blood. 'It just feels weird, I guess. You're going to give me a kidney and I didn't even know that you play chess.'

'Would you prefer a kidney from someone who played Scrabble?'

Holly laughed. 'It's not something I'd even be thinking about if it was an anonymous donor.'

'Wouldn't you?' Ryan looked curious. 'If it was me, I think I'd end up wondering rather a lot about where it had come from. What kind of person the previous owner had been.'

Holly thought about the request she'd seen on the organ matching website, that the recipient have the chance to get to know the donor and vice versa. And the interview clip where the relationship between donor and recipient had become as close as family.

How close was this going to make her and Ryan?

He must have picked up on her speculation. 'You're welcome to know as much—or as little—as you want to know about me, Holly.' He gestured towards the impressive row of test tubes she was picking up to go into the path lab bag. 'If my health is the only concern, you should get all the answers you need from that lot.' He slid off the bed and plucked a roll of tape from the top of the trolley. 'And I'm fit. Going to my fencing club once a week takes care of that.'

Holly sealed the top of the plastic bag. 'Fencing?'

'You really think I'm strange now, don't you?'

'Um…' Holly held onto the bag without moving to drop it into the collection tray. 'Are we talking farm fencing or pickets?'

'Neither. Sport fencing. You know, swordfighting?'

Holly just stared at him, completely at a loss for words at this latest revelation from her boss.

'I don't compete or anything.' Ryan was fiddling with the length of tape as he stuck it to the swab covering his puncture site. 'It's just a fitness thing. It's physically challenging and you have to use your brain at the same time.' His glance was slightly defensive. 'Not really so strange. I heard someone refer to it once as chess at a hundred miles an hour.' He shrugged. 'I guess rock 'n' roll dancing would do the job just as well but you need a partner for that.'

'Oh, I'd *love* to be able to dance!'

The words came from nowhere. Holly barely had the energy to walk some days and a conscious desire to do any form of dancing had never surfaced coherently. Something fundamental in her life seemed to have changed in the last few hours and it was unsettling.

So was the rather speculative gleam in Ryan's eye.

'Tell you what,' he said. 'Let's make a deal. When we're both back on our feet after all this, we'll see if we can find a dance class to get really fit again. Rock 'n' roll—or would you prefer Latin?'

'Um…' A sudden image of dancing a tango with Ryan flashed into Holly's brain and she could feel a faint sense of panic at the bizarre, if not altogether unpleasant, notion.

Learning to live with her illness had meant careful planning and organisation. Being impulsive or 'going with the flow' was alien to Holly but she felt like she was being swept along on some current right now. A current that was being generated by the man who had clearly just noticed her discomfort.

'It's not a prerequisite or anything,' he said lightly. 'Don't worry. It was just a thought.' Ryan checked his watch. 'It's time we headed home, I think. Big day tomorrow.'

'Mmm.' It was a relief to switch to familiar discussion ground. 'I want to read up on transposition of the great arteries so I know exactly what you're doing with Grace tomorrow.'

Not that Holly would be assisting with this major surgery, which could take many hours. The consultant from the other paediatric cardiac surgery team would be working with Ryan this time, but Holly would get to watch and that was exciting enough.

The next couple of days would be full on, what with Grace's surgery and with Leo still in Intensive Care after his successful operation today, but that was a good thing. Holly felt a distinct need to ground herself before taking the next step in the journey she had embarked on by agreeing to the kidney transplant. She went home, determined to focus on nothing but the upcoming stint in the operating theatre the next day.

Ryan's initial offer had been enough to start her wondering about his personal life. Now that she'd agreed to accept that offer, she was discovering things that were downright startling. There was no denying a desire to bolt back to a place where Ryan was primarily a surgeon again and several hours of standing on her feet while the congenital abnormality in tiny Grace's heart was repaired should make that desire quite achievable.

It wasn't working.

Being a spectator rather than an active participant didn't help. It gave Holly's concentration far too many opportunities to slip. And the frequent glances coming her way from the personnel crowding Theatre made it virtually impossible to focus for long.

It was her own fault. Holly had arrived early that morning to be present at the final preparatory review of the case and found she had beaten the second surgeon, Colin. Ryan had been pleased to have a moment to themselves because he'd had a question for her.

'How private do you want to keep this transplant business, Holly? Only I'm going to have to have a word with Colin about cover. We can postpone any elective cases easily enough but emergencies are a different story and I'll need some co-operation to bring my annual leave forward.'

Holly had searched his face but hadn't found any clues about what his preference might be. 'I think privacy is a luxury that can go straight out the window when medical professionals have medical procedures. Will it bother you that people know?'

'Not if it doesn't bother you. I'm more than happy to be open about it.'

'Me, too.' Holly's nod had been resigned. 'It's not as if people don't already know about my state of health.'

So Ryan had talked to Colin and Colin had said something to his registrar who happened to be dating the scrub nurse on duty that morning so it had taken a matter of minutes for the news to get passed to her. They had been overheard by the technician setting up the heart-lung machine and by the time they had all been ready to shift their focus to the major task ahead, the only person who hadn't known had been the anaesthetist who'd been in the anteroom with baby Grace. He'd managed to get clued up somehow despite his attention to his own tasks.

'Congratulations,' he whispered hurriedly to Holly when she moved past. 'Fantastic news!'

The level of interest didn't surprise Holly at all. She'd been through it once before when last month's potential transplant had disrupted her working week. But the depth of interest this time was so much greater because another colleague was also involved and the potential for success was also higher. The pleasure she could sense on her behalf was something of a revelation and, judging by those frequent glances coming her way, they would all be eager for more information and progress reports.

It was easy initially to push personal concerns aside as the surgery began. Baby Grace's tiny chest was opened and the sternum retracted. The membrane around her heart was divided and then sutured to the surrounding stockinette wound towels to elevate the heart for better exposure. Ryan and Colin spent some time carefully assessing the coronary anatomy, using marking sutures to indicate the intended positions of the coronary arterial openings. The baby's body was cooled to a temperature of less than twenty degrees Centigrade and cardiopulmonary bypass was started.

For a long while, even Ryan's favourite Vivaldi CD did little to counteract a tense atmosphere as the intricate surgery progressed. Holly had never seen a procedure quite like it. Tiny buttons of flesh and string-sized vessels were cut free, repositioned and sewn into place with the most precise stitches Holly had ever seen Ryan perform. She couldn't see into the actual field of surgery from where she stood, but the camera in the magnifying goggles Ryan wore sent the images to a large screen on one side of the high-tech operating theatre.

Thus distanced, it was too easy for part of her mind to start playing truant—thinking about Ryan the man rather than the surgeon. The information she had gained so recently was changing her perspective an astonishing amount. She watched the almost negligible cuts being made with a razor-sharp scalpel and wondered if the amount of control needed got somehow replenished when Ryan indulged in his hobby of swinging a large sword at an opponent. Was his fencing an instinctive form of gaining balance in his life as much as a small boy's dream technique of keeping fit?

Maybe she should try it for herself when she felt fit enough?

Maybe she should even take up Ryan's offer of being a dance partner?

Then again, maybe she should just concentrate on her career and try not to let herself get so distracted by the upcoming changes in her life—particularly ones that were based on the oddly new habit of fantasy rather than the well-rehearsed practice of dealing with reality.

The last pantaloon-shaped piece of pericardial tissue was sutured into place to cover the defects the surgical technique had created, and the slow business of discontinuing bypass began. Finally, all suture lines were covered with a fibrin glue. Holly was pleased when the surgeons decided that primary closure of the sternum could be tolerated. Having the chest wall left open even temporarily would have made it far more traumatic for Grace's parents in the immediate post-operative period.

As it was, their baby would be kept heavily sedated and on a ventilator for twenty-four to forty-eight hours, with a barrage of medication to support her through the recovery period. The outlook was good, however, with a high survival rate, and Ryan and Colin would soon be able to break the family's tense wait with the news that the surgery had gone extremely well.

The news of Holly's own upcoming surgery was the talk of the whole of St Margaret's within a few hours of baby Grace being transferred to the surgical ICU. Holly's friend on the nursing staff in the unit, Sue, found her in the ward late that afternoon when Ryan was meeting with Colin to dictate their surgical notes on the morning's case.

Her expression was enough to make Holly's heart skip a beat.

'What is it, Sue? Is Grace in trouble?'

'No, she's a wee fighter, that one. She's doing fantastically well so far.'

'Is it Leo, then?'

'No, no. He woke up for a minute not long ago and smiled at his mum. She's rapt.' Sue's eyes were suspiciously bright as she gave Holly an impulsive hug. 'I've just heard about you and Ryan and I'm so happy for you. Congratulations! When's the big day going to be?'

Holly almost winced. 'You make it sound like we've just got engaged.'

Sue laughed. 'I did, didn't I?' Her glance, as she stepped back, held an edge of curiosity that Holly knew she would encounter again as the news spread. Sue knew perfectly well that there was no man in Holly's life but how many people would assume that there had to be something more than a working relationship between her and Ryan?

Should she set out to make things clear? Ryan had said he was happy to be open about the transplant but that might not include having his motivation discussed. Holly hadn't known he was a widower. That he'd tried, and failed, to make a physical contribution to save his wife's life. People might accept that as motivation enough, as Holly had done, thinking that by helping someone else like this might be helping Ryan to exorcise a painful ghost from his own life. But if Ryan wanted that to be common knowledge, that was his business. He had to be fielding as much interest as she was.

What was he telling everybody?

Holly found out, a short time later, when Ryan arrived to check her notes on Daniel.

'He's so keen to get home. And back to school. Sounds like he's a real hero now that he's been on TV. He's been up and down the stairs with the physio today with no problems.'

'We can look at discharge in the next day or two.'

'Apparently Sox gave him some tickets to the next Blues

game in a couple of weeks. I said he'd have to talk to you about whether he'll be able to go.'

Ryan smiled. 'I'd better go and give him the good news, then. Nothing like having something to look forward to, to help speed up recovery. Speaking of which...' Ryan raised an eyebrow '...are you being bombarded with questions about what we've both got to look forward to?'

Holly nodded. 'The grapevine is humming, that's for sure.'

'Getting to you?'

'A bit. I'm not sure what I should say when people want to ask me about why you're doing this.'

'Just tell them what I'm telling them.'

'Which is?'

'That, by some happy coincidence, we've turned out to be a perfect match.' Ryan's gaze was oddly serious. 'That's all they need to know, Holly. Anything else is between you and me.'

So he didn't want people to know his personal history. The phrase was nicely ambiguous, though, wasn't it? Holly could just imagine it fuelling gossip that there was more than a blood or tissue type match being referred to. She wasn't about to point that out to Ryan, however. How embarrassed would he be to know that she was even thinking along such lines?

'Have you heard from Doug?' Ryan queried as he reached for Daniel's notes. 'About the meeting with the transplant team?'

'They've pencilled in a slot for 3 p.m. tomorrow. It looks clear in our schedules but I said I'd check with you.' Holly caught her breath. 'Things seem to be moving a bit fast. We don't have to rush this if you'd rather wait, Ryan.'

'The sooner the better, as far as I'm concerned.'

Holly's gazed rested on his profile for a moment as he scanned her notes on the physical examination she had made on Daniel. Of course he would want to get it out of the way. Maybe he was aware of the potential gossip and found it intrusive. The sooner life was back to normal, the better.

It was more like an interdepartmental meeting than a patient-doctor interview.

Doug Smiley, two transplant surgeons, Holly and Ryan sat drinking coffee as they discussed her case.

'You'll both be well aware of the mechanics of the surgery. Your op will take two to four hours, Holly. You'll get an incision of around twenty centimetres, lower abdomen.' The surgeon winked. 'I'll make sure I keep it low enough for the scar not to show on the beach when you're wearing your bikini.'

'Not a problem, Ken. I might dream of a day or two lazing on a beach but I haven't managed it in about six years so I don't think it's a major consideration.'

'I'll keep it pretty anyway. You'll get the renal artery and vein of the new kidney connected to a main artery and vein in your pelvis, and the ureter will be connected to your bladder. We went over all this not so long ago, didn't we?'

Holly nodded. 'I'll have a Foley catheter in for a few days and I shouldn't expect to be producing urine immediately. It's no biggie if I need dialysis to start with.'

'We'll expect to be discharging you in seven to ten days.'

The other surgeon looked at Ryan. 'You probably won't need to be in that long. With laparoscopic surgery and being as fit as you are, you might find you can get home by day five.'

'Great. I'm arranging a two- to three-week cover period in any case.'

'Doug said you weren't keen to talk to the counsellor we've got on our team.'

'No. I'm well acquainted with any risk statistics.'

'And the possibility that the transplant might not succeed?'

Ryan just smiled. 'As far as I'm concerned, the potential benefits outweigh any risks by a country mile. I'm quite happy with my decision and I don't need to take up any counsellor's time.'

'Neither do I,' Holly added.

Both surgeons nodded. 'We'll need you both in the day before surgery for a final physical check and the fluid loading. Holly, you'll need longer because we'll be giving you a dialysis session and getting you started on your immunosuppressive medication about twelve hours prior to surgery.'

'What will you use?' Ryan asked with interest.

'Cyclosporin A to start with. We'll kick off with a high dose of about 10 to 15 milligrams per kilogram a day and then reduce it to a maintenance dose hopefully low enough to avoid side effects. We might have to juggle with other immunosuppressants or corticosteroids for a while until we get things just right. Doug will be taking care of that side of things.'

Doug smiled at Holly. 'I intend to make it my mission to ensure you don't grow a beard, become obese or get a bad tremor.'

'Thanks.' Unless she had to, Holly didn't want to cross the bridge of unwanted side effects to drugs she would have to be taking for the rest of her life. 'I'll hold you to that, Doug.'

'Anything else either of you want to know?'

'Yes,' Ryan said. 'How about giving us a date?'

'Would next week be too soon?' Ken queried. 'We've both got a morning free in Theatre.'

'No,' Ryan said.

'*Yes*,' Holly said with a note of panic she couldn't suppress. Then she looked at Ryan, caught his gaze for several seconds and received a wave of reassurance. It was that dialysis effect again, which sent fears and doubts out the window and instilled confidence…and hope.

It was hard to break the eye contact, even knowing that its length could transmit the wrong message to the other people present. Holly took a deep breath and forced herself to look away from Ryan.

'I meant no,' she said as firmly as she could. 'Next week would be just fine.'

Ryan had been watching her all through her evaluation of baby Grace's condition.

'No significant change from this morning. She's quite stable,' Holly reported with satisfaction. 'All her vital signs are within normal limits. Oxygen saturation is a hundred per cent and she's in sinus rhythm with a good rate. Blood pressure's fine, urine output's good and the wound's clean. We could think about weaning her off the ventilator now, couldn't we?'

'Absolutely.'

'And Leo's ready to go to the ward.'

'He's looking good, isn't he? I'll have a chat to Mum and make sure she's ready for the move.'

Looking up from charting the new plan of treatment for Grace, Holly wasn't surprised to see Leo's mother, Bianca, looking anxious. The one-on-one nursing and all the high-tech equipment available in the intensive care unit were very reassuring for many parents. They could easily keep Leo here for another day if necessary.

She saw Ryan reach out to touch Bianca's arm but the gesture didn't seem to be one of reassurance. The surgeon looked as though he was clutching Bianca's arm, and Leo's mother was looking progressively more anxious. Sue was standing beside the bed and her expression as she stared at her patient's mother was one of sheer disbelief.

Holly scribbled her signature on Grace's chart and moved swiftly to the door in the glass walls of Leo's cubicle. What on earth was being said in there?

Ryan glanced up as she entered but he was busy helping Bianca to sit down. On the floor, of all places! Was she feeling faint?

'Grab some towels, would you, please, Sue?' Ryan stretched over Bianca's head to pull some gloves from the box over the handbasin.

Holly could see why the towels were needed. Something had been spilled on the floor. The puddle was large...and growing.

'Oh!' Being the end of a busy day wasn't really enough of an excuse that she'd taken so long to click, but this was hardly an expected occurrence in the paediatric surgical ICU. 'Your waters have broken, Bianca. Should I find a stretcher, Ryan?'

'I doubt we have time for a transfer.' Ryan had lifted the hem of Bianca's maternity dress and, over his shoulder, Holly could see the shape of part of a baby through the thin fabric of a pair of very wet knickers. 'When did you last deliver a baby, Holly?'

'I can't have it *now*,' Bianca gasped. 'Not *here*!'

'You had a scan done yesterday, didn't you?' Holly found a pair of scissors on the tray of the nearby dressings trolley and handed them to Ryan.

'Yes. And the baby had turned around. I thought that might be why things felt a bit funny today. I was going to call my midwife once Leo's dad came back to sit with him.' Bianca took another gasping, inward breath. 'Ooh, I'm getting another contraction.'

If the baby had turned itself around yesterday, the position hadn't been held. What Holly and Ryan could see clearly, as the fabric was cut free, was a pair of tiny buttocks.

The obstetrics Holly had done seemed a very long time ago and she'd only ever assisted once at a breech birth. The potential for disaster was much higher than with a normal presentation. Horror stories of entrapment of the head, brain damage and even death crowded Holly's thoughts. Leo's parents had quite enough to cope with right now, without adding major complications from a difficult delivery of his sibling.

This was a paediatric hospital. They might have any number of paediatricians used to dealing with newborn babies but there were no obstetric specialists on the staff. Holly had to fight back a major dose of nerves.

Ryan, however, appeared perfectly calm. 'You're doing just fine, Bianca. She's a few weeks early so I suspect she'll be small enough to make this easy.'

Sue appeared back with an armload of clean, fluffy towels. 'We've got a team and an incubator on their way up from Neonates.'

'Excellent.' Ryan was cradling the presenting part of the baby and first one leg and then the other appeared.

Leo stirred and whimpered at that point. He was still under sedation for pain control but Sue moved to check on the toddler. Bianca groaned and Holly crouched to hold her hand. She gave it a squeeze.

'It's all good,' she said reassuringly. 'Sue's looking after Leo and Ryan knows what he's doing.'

He certainly seemed to, anyway. Tiny legs were held between the gloved fingers of one hand while the other supported the rest of the baby. She saw him move his hands, carefully holding the body as it turned one way and then the other to allow delivery of the shoulders and arms.

There was a small lull as Ryan waited for another contraction to help the delivery of the baby's head. Holly could see the intense concentration on his face—absolute determination to do this exactly right—and because she was watching him just as intently, she saw the moment anxiety gave way to relief as he lifted the baby clear.

Ryan was watching the baby, keeping it tilted down to help keep the airway clear. The suction tubing Sue had detached from the wall unit and was clutching on the other side of the bed wasn't needed. The baby's arms moved and then its face, scrunching into lines of dismay before a tiny mouth opened to take its first breath and emit a warbling cry.

But Holly didn't see the baby's face. She was still watching the man who had just completed the unexpected delivery of this infant and she saw the joy that now softened his features. Ryan looked up then, lifting the baby to place her on her mother's stomach but his glance stopped as it caught Holly's.

And then the whole world seemed to stop.

There were tears in Ryan's eyes. Hardly surprising, given the emotion of the moment. Holly was feeling choked up herself and Bianca was laughing and sobbing at the same time as she reached to touch her baby. The touch of Ryan's gaze with Holly's lasted only a split second but its aftermath made everything happening from then on seem hazy.

The team from the neonatal unit arrived seconds later and Leo's room was a scene of happy chaos as they took over the care of a small but apparently healthy baby girl. Holly helped set up the incubator as a paediatrician examined the baby, whose cries were amazingly not enough to wake her older brother. Ryan dealt with the delivery of the placenta and Sue went to summon an ambulance crew to transfer Bianca to the maternity unit at Auckland General Hospital for the check she would need. Leo's father arrived at the same time as the ambulance crew and Holly stood back as the chaos finally receded.

Remarkably, it had all occurred in the space of less than thirty minutes. That moment of eye contact with Ryan had lasted less than a second but Holly still couldn't shake the feeling of connection it had given her. The warmth that had been generated was still with her. So was that odd sensation of tightness in her chest and stomach. Holly had not experienced that sensation for a very long time, but it was all too easily recognisable.

You could only get that feeling with someone who was as close as it was possible to get with another person.

With someone you were in love with.

Was this a result of sharing a rather extraordinary experience with Ryan in the last half-hour? Being blown away by his presence of mind and skill and his emotional involvement with the situation?

Or was it because she'd been seeing him in such a different and more personal light over the last few days?

Or was it simply a form of gratitude for what he was preparing to do for her with such generosity of spirit?

Or had all of these circumstances combined to open a door to a space that had actually been there all along? A closed door that Holly had simply walked past in her mind on countless occasions, never for one moment considering that she had the opportunity to open it.

Leo's cubicle was clear now, except for Sue who was busy taking a set of routine vital sign measurements on the peacefully sleeping toddler. And Ryan was still there, of course.

He was looking at Holly. And smiling.

'That was a bit different,' he said dryly. 'Life's full of surprises, isn't it?'

Holly could do nothing but return the smile and nod.

And thank her lucky stars that Ryan Murphy was not privy to the extra surprise life had just handed her.

CHAPTER FIVE

IT WOULDN'T last.

A night of reflection had convinced Holly that the new feelings she had discovered for Ryan were a perfectly understandable reaction to the physical and emotional journey he was responsible for her having embarked on.

Negative emotions like fear and frustration and despair were being nudged out of long-term occupancy in her life to make way for genuine hope. For the first time in years Holly could think about a future beyond getting through her day or her next dialysis session and past being simply a slot on a waiting list for a transplant organ.

She was very careful to keep her interaction with Ryan as professional as possible over the next couple of days. A new fear had been spawned, in fact. What if Ryan thought he could be stuck with a love-sick registrar because he'd offered to save her life? It could well be enough to make him reconsider.

To back out.

Hard to believe it was only a matter of days since Holly had dismissed Ryan's offer as being stunning but ridiculous. Now, with surgery only days away, the thought of the offer being withdrawn was terrifying. Holly was on the biggest emotional roller-coaster of her life right now. Feelings for Ryan had to go into one of those carriages. A passenger on the ride that was probably not even strapped in.

It wouldn't last.

There was something different about the way Holly was looking at him but that was hardly surprising. Ryan knew she must be feeling grateful and he couldn't forget what she'd said initially about gratitude being a burden that could damage their professional relationship so maybe that oddly thoughtful expression he seemed to be catching so frequently was indicative of mixed emotions on her part.

He sighed inwardly, wishing he could find a way to make all this easier for Holly, and the sigh took on an extra dimension as he eyed what was inside the container Holly was opening. A rather wilted and unattractive-looking salad that had lumps of what looked like tuna in it was clearly her only lunch for the day. No wonder Holly didn't seem very interested in her food. She eyed the bag Ryan was carrying into his office.

'That smells good. Did you go for those hot bacon and egg sandwiches again?'

'Mmm.' Ryan sat down on the other side of his desk, nudging the pile of case notes they were intending to review in their lunch-break to one side. 'I've got heaps. Want one?'

Holly shook her head sadly. 'High salt. You heard me promise Doug I'd pay particular attention to my diet this week. If I ate them I'd get thirsty and then I might throw my whole fluid balance out.'

'You're a model patient, aren't you?' Ryan felt slightly guilty as he laid the bag flat and ripped it open to release even more of the fragrant smell of fried bacon.

'I have to be,' Holly said matter-of-factly. 'It's been hard enough without making things worse by breaking the rules.'

'Well, apart from having to remember your anti-rejection medication, the rules should slacken quite a lot once you've got a functioning new kidney.'

Holly grimaced as she poked at her salad with a plastic fork. 'I can't wait.'

'You won't have to wait much longer.' Ryan didn't need to glance at his desk calendar with the day now circled in red. 'Only four days to go.'

'Mmm.' Holly's fork was chasing a lump of tuna through the lettuce bed.

'Nervous?'

'A little.' Dark eyes flashed up to meet his briefly. 'Are you?'

'No.' Ryan took another bite of his sandwich. 'Not a bit.' Not for himself, anyway, but Holly seemed too frail to be about to undergo major surgery. Ryan's gaze was caught by the way the bone on the edge of her wrist glowed white under her skin as she moved her fork. 'You look like you've lost a bit of weight, Holly. You're not overdoing your exercise programme, are you?'

'I'm not doing any more than usual. Walking to and from work is it really.'

'You don't walk in this sort of weather, do you? It's pouring today.'

'I have a good umbrella.' Holly looked up again and smiled. ' We live in Auckland, Ryan. You'd be mad *not* to have a good umbrella.'

'I'll give you a lift home today if it's still raining.'

'No need. Thanks, anyway.'

'You don't want to have to postpone surgery because

you've got yourself cold and wet and picked up some kind of virus. There's a lot of bugs around at this time of year. You need rest.' Ryan looked pointedly at Holly's lunch. 'And good food.'

'You do have a point.' Holly grinned. 'Is that offer of a sandwich still open, then? The smell is driving me crazy.'

The pleasure gained from seeing Holly taking such an enthusiastic bite of the thick sandwich was startlingly intense. When a drop of egg yolk escaped at the corner of her mouth, it was all Ryan could do not to reach out and catch it with his thumb. Things had changed all right. A week ago he would never have allowed such a notion to enter his head. Now he had to actively seek distraction.

He cleared his throat. 'Did you see Leo's dad when he came in for a visit this morning?'

'No. He had his grandma keeping him company.'

'The baby's fine, by the sound of it. Pretty small but healthy enough. She's in an incubator for a few days to be sure and she'll have to stay in hospital until she reaches a good birth weight, but it's good news, isn't it?'

Holly only paused briefly before taking another bite of her sandwich. 'Absolutely.'

'How about Michaela? Did you manage to find time for your usual visit?'

'Just a quick one.'

'Sounds like they've got her renal function back in control.'

'Yes, but her heart failure's getting worse. If they let her go home, she's going to be confined to a wheelchair or her bed.'

'Her family seem desperate to get her back home as soon as possible. Will they cope, do you think?'

'What choice do they have?'

'Hmm.' The distraction of discussing patients wasn't working. Ryan's thoughts had just done another neat circle back to Holly. 'How are you planning to cope after your discharge?'

'I guess I'll need a quiet week or two at home.'

'Who's going to be looking after you?'

Holly shrugged. 'I can look after myself, Ryan. I have done for years. You know that.'

'But this is different.'

'Why? It's not as if they'll be discharging me before I'm able to get around easily. I've got it all planned. I'm going to spend this weekend putting meals in the freezer so I won't have to cook, and I'm going to the library to get a load of books. I'm looking forward to having a fiction-fest for a change. Total indulgence, in fact. I might get a whole stack of historical romances.'

Ryan wasn't satisfied. 'You shouldn't be on your own. Haven't you got friends or family you could stay with?'

'Dad lives in Sydney, close to my brother. They've invited me to go over there to recuperate but Liz, my sister-in-law, has a fairly new baby and she helps Dad out a lot so she's got enough on her hands.'

'What about having a friend to stay? Like Sue?'

'Sue's got her own family to take care of. Besides, my apartment is only designed to have one person living in it. I've got plenty of neighbours, Ryan. And a telephone. I'll be fine.'

'You could stay with us.' The words popped out and startled Ryan almost as much as they apparently startled Holly. She nearly dropped her fork.

'*Us*?'

That was strange. Ryan could swear the tone was one of dismay. 'Me and Pop.'

'You live with your grandfather?'

'Kind of. It's a huge old house and it got divided when Pop's son—my father—got married. It's really two separate houses but we try and make an effort to see each other every day. I moved in when I first came back to Auckland and there's never been a good reason to move out. Pop would deny it ferociously, of course, but he does need someone keeping a bit of an eye on him.'

'I can understand that. How old did you say he was?'

'Ninety-six.' Ryan smiled. 'But he's a great cook. I pretend I can't live without his food and he pretends he just puts up with me and doesn't rely on my company. It works well.'

'He sounds like a bit of a character.'

'He is. He'd like to meet you, by the way. What would you say to a home-cooked meal tonight? One that doesn't have any rabbit food in sight?'

Holly laughed. 'I'd say that I've already wrecked my diet enough for one day.'

She was curious, though. Ryan was getting that thoughtful look again.

'What about roast lamb?' he queried cunningly. 'With mint sauce and gravy and baby peas and itty-bitty new potatoes?'

'Ooh…' The sound was almost a groan of desire, and did something very strange to Ryan's stomach. Then Holly's eyes narrowed suspiciously. 'How did you know that's my all-time favourite dinner? It's what we always had on Christmas Day.'

'I didn't. It just happens to be one of Pop's specialities. He cooks the leg of lamb in a clay case that keeps it all juicy and he grows fresh mint to make his own sauce and puts it in with the potatoes and—'

'Stop!' Holly was laughing. 'I don't believe you, anyway. Itty-bitty new potatoes in the middle of winter? I don't think so!'

'Pop has his sources. He was a chef until he ended up owning his own restaurant.' Suddenly it was important to Ryan that Holly visited his home and met his only family, but he tried to keep his tone casual. 'Hey, we're both going to be eating hospital food for at least a week. We owe it to ourselves to indulge a bit first.'

He'd like to tell her that she needed some lovingly prepared food that might actually put a decent covering on those bones. That he had every intention of seeing her healthy and cared for as much as he was able to. But Ryan knew not to push any further. He was taking another step over personal-life boundary lines here and, having issued the invitation, it was time to back off and let Holly think about it.

He pushed his shirtsleeve up to expose his watch. 'I guess we'd better have a quick look over these notes so we've got some idea of who's coming to our outpatient clinic this afternoon.'

The clinic that afternoon was for the purpose of seeing potential elective surgical cases rather than a follow-up of post-operative patients, but the first appointment managed to fit both categories.

'Our GP referred us to the cardiology department in Wellington where we've been living, but when they said that Bella probably needed surgery, we asked if we could come and see you, Dr Murphy—seeing as you operated on Bella when she was a baby.'

Ryan smiled at the eight-year-old girl sitting between her parents. 'You won't remember me,' he said, 'but I remember you. You were just this big.' He held his hands about eighteen inches apart.

'How old was I?'

'About three weeks.'

'And what was wrong with me?' Bella's stare suggested that she wasn't the least bit shy.

'You had something we call pulmonary stenosis,' Ryan explained. 'Your heart has things called valves in it and one of your valves didn't grow quite the way it should have before you were born.'

Bella cut straight to the chase. 'Why didn't you fix it up properly, then?'

'Bella!' Her mother looked embarrassed but Ryan smiled again.

'We tried our best,' he told the girl seriously. 'But sometimes, when children grow, the problem can come back.'

'Is that what's happened to me?'

'That's why you're coming to see us. We need to find that out.'

'If it has happened to me, can you fix it up this time?'

'Yes,' Ryan said confidently.

Bella's nod was satisfied and Ryan looked up to include her parents in the interview. 'Our referral letter says that you took Bella to your GP because she's been getting tired rather easily, is that right?'

Bella's mother nodded. 'She's too tired to even eat her dinner some nights.'

'She gets short of breath,' her father added. 'And last week, when she was out running around with our new puppy, she said she got a really bad pain in her chest.'

'According to the records from the GP, Bella has been well up to now. She hasn't had any other major illnesses or problems and her vaccinations are all up to date. Correct?'

'Yes.'

'And you've been living in Wellington for a few years now?'

'We're thinking of moving back to Auckland. Most of our family's up here.'

Bella was starting to look bored. She swung small feet and kicked the legs of her chair. Then she stared at Holly, who was sitting near Ryan.

'You've got really long hair,' Bella stated.

'I have, haven't I?' Holly kept her voice down so as not to interrupt the history Ryan was still going over with Bella's parents. 'That's why I have to keep it in a plait when I'm at work.'

Bella fingered a blonde pigtail that didn't quite reach her shoulder. 'Jessie bites my hair.'

'Is Jessie your new puppy?'

'Yeah. Are you a heart doctor, too?'

'I sure am.'

'I'm going to be a animal doctor when I grow up.'

'Cool.'

'I'm going to practise on Jessie.'

'Oh…' Holly made a mental note to revisit the subject at a later date on Jessie's behalf. Ryan had stopped making notes now and it was time for a physical examination for Bella. Then they would review the recent chest X-rays, echocardiogram and blood tests that had been done in Wellington. Judging by the letter she and Ryan had gone over in their lunch-break and the snippets she had overheard of this interview, it seemed highly likely that Bella would be one of their first surgical patients when she and Ryan returned from sick leave.

Thoughts about that leave intruded more than once during the hours of that clinic. Holly felt she couldn't possibly accept Ryan's offer of a place to stay during her recuperation but he had, inadvertently perhaps, opened a rather large can of worms.

Only half her mind was on the interview with the next patient's family. The girl had been diagnosed with an atrial septal defect at birth. She had never exhibited any symptoms but her mother had been on the internet to learn of possible complications, such as heart failure or arrhythmias, that her daughter could face in her forties or fifties.

'Wouldn't it be better to have surgery and repair the defect now?' she asked Ryan.

'Open heart surgery isn't something to take lightly,' he responded. 'Fleur is a well, happy child at the moment and investigations suggest that the defect is relatively small. This is her chest X-ray here, see? With a defect likely to cause problems later in life, we'd expect to see a much larger heart size, with a prominent atrium and pulmonary artery. Just here.' Ryan was using a pen to point to the viewing screen just behind his chair. 'Fleur's are a little enlarged but not enough to make me concerned. And this is her ECG.' He pulled the page from the child's file and began an explanation of the results in terms designed for lay people to comprehend.

Holly's concentration wandered, dipping into that worm can again. Loneliness had been a fact of life ever since the struggle to keep up her career had made trying to socialise more of an ordeal than a pleasure. Her circle of friends had dwindled to those she saw at work and they all worked long hours themselves and many had their own families to go home to by now. Days off were normally taken up with coping with housework, laundry and grocery shopping, with any surplus energy being channelled into study. Sheer exhaustion and the demands of her home treatment had disguised how alone Holly was most of the time, but that was about to change.

Holly was actually dreading the days alone in her apartment after discharge more than the surgery or hospital stay. If the transplant was successful, she would have more energy than she'd had for years. Long hours in every day to find something to do.

Alone.

Fleur left, with her parents totally reassured by the promise of continued monitoring of their daughter's heart condition. Her place was taken by a six-month-old baby whom they had expected to need surgery for a large ventricular septal defect that had been causing quite marked symptoms only three months ago. Medical treatment had been effective for control, however, and the baby's growth had led to a partial closure of the defect. She was still borderline for surgical intervention, and Ryan was happy to agree with the parents' request that they wait a bit longer. With a bit of luck, the defect would close even further and they could look forward to a healthy future for their child without the need for major surgery.

Holly was looking forward to a healthy future herself but right now a part of it was looming as a scarily empty void and a period of recuperation from major surgery was not going to be the time to try and get out and about, renewing or making new friendships, was it? Ryan's new offer was, once again, so tempting that Holly's mind refused to leave it alone.

A huge house, he'd said.

But not an empty one. If she stayed there, she'd have company. The support of someone going through a similar period of recuperation, no less. A medical professional who might be a great insurance policy just in case some nasty complication reared its head, like her spiking enough of a fever to make her delirious or getting a scare like passing blood in her urine.

Not that she expected any such complications, of course. Her mind was just craftily dreaming up a reasonable excuse to spend more time with Ryan. Holly could recognise what was happening, but wasn't convinced she had the motivation to put up enough of a fight.

Given her confused feelings about Ryan at present, it would be a huge mistake to share a house and risk being drawn even closer. What if she *really* fell in love with him? She'd have to cope with getting over him on top of all the other challenges she would face in the near future.

The final patient for the clinic that day was a fifteen-month-old boy called Thomas who had been diagnosed with coarctation of the aorta after his GP had picked up a heart murmur on a routine check prior to an immunisation. Thomas had a young, single mother and it was her father who had come to the appointment as support. Thomas's grandfather.

How could Holly help but start wondering about Ryan's grandfather? The idea of a ninety-six-year-old who was a gourmet cook, grew his own herbs and was still sharp enough to win at chess was intriguing. He had to be a bit special, too. How many men of Ryan's age would care enough to check on the welfare of an elderly relative every day?

Or was it Ryan that was the special one?

Thomas was unfazed by the appointment that was deciding a date for the surgery he needed. He trotted back and forth across the consulting room, choosing toys from the large basket in the corner and then taking each item to offer, with some awe, to Ryan. The surgeon's lap was already crowded with wooden blocks, plastic stacking rings, a toy aeroplane and a Barbie doll, but that didn't stop him thanking Thomas for the knitted elephant that appeared next.

And then he looked across at Holly and smiled with just a hint of a wink creasing the corner of one eye. Other doctors who could see the finishing post for a busy afternoon's clinic might well have been irritated by the constant interruptions to an important conversation, but Ryan was actually enjoying the interaction with this small boy.

And he wanted Holly to share that enjoyment.

It was the kind of sharing that made life that much more meaningful. The kind of communication that came automatically when you were in the company of someone you got on well with. Holly knew, in that moment, that if Ryan made another offer of company when she was discharged from hospital, she'd already lost the strength to decline, no matter how many sensible warnings the rational part of her brain could issue.

She hoped he would reissue the invitation. She was hoping it again when Ryan led the way out of the outpatient department just before 6 p.m.

'So…' He waved at the receptionist, tidying magazines in the waiting area. 'What do you think?'

'Um…' With a start, Holly realised she hadn't heard the last thing Ryan had said. She'd been too busy wondering if he might use the time walking out of the department to return to their lunchtime conversation.

'You haven't heard a word I've been saying, have you?' Ryan didn't sound annoyed, though. 'I'm talking about operating on someone with a right ventricular pressure of less than a hundred millimetres mercury.'

'Um…' Holly did her best to concentrate. 'You mean Bella? I'd say she's certainly symptomatic enough for surgery to be indicated, no matter what her pressure or gradient is.'

Ryan was silent, as though expecting Holly to expand on her answer, but for once in her life Holly was not particularly interested in pursuing a professional discussion. She could feel the quizzical glance she received.

'I've had the feeling you've had some other things on your mind this afternoon, Holly.'

'Oh, was it that obvious? Sorry, Ryan.'

'It's quite understandable.' He held the door open for her. 'You were thinking about the possibility of a roast lamb dinner, yes?'

Holly grinned. 'How did you guess?'

'I didn't.' The door swung shut behind them with a puff of cool air. 'But I'm glad I rang Pop before clinic and told him he'd better set an extra place, just in case.'

'That was the best dinner I've ever eaten in my entire life.'

Jack Murphy shrugged off the compliment with a gesture that was so like his grandson that Holly had to smile.

'You were just hungry, that's all. You need feeding, girl. Turn you sideways and you'd disappear off the radar.'

'It was great, Pop.' Ryan pushed his plate away and sighed with contentment. 'Thanks.'

'He only lives here because he's too lazy to cook for himself,' Jack informed Holly. 'Don't know why I put up with him.'

Holly felt like she'd been smiling continuously ever since she'd arrived at the Murphy household. The bond and affection between these two men was obviously very deep. And the notion that Ryan would end up very like Jack in sixty years or so was fascinating. Jack might have lost a few inches in height but he was still impressively tall and he had a thick thatch of white hair that was just as shaggy as Ryan's tawny mop. He gave off the same aura of kindness as well. His delight in Holly coming to visit couldn't have been anything other than genuine.

'The lad's told me all about you,' he'd said. 'Mind you, I think he was just trying to put me off my game so he could win for once. Never stops talking, that boy. Don't know why I put up with him. You need a bit of peace and quiet at my age, y'know.'

Clearly revelling in a new audience, Jack had continued an almost solid wall of talking as he'd led Holly into the house. Driving in through what appeared to be acres of dark garden to arrive at this wonderful old house that sat within a short stroll to the beach of Herne Bay had been somewhat overwhelming for Holly, but within minutes of being in Jack's company she had felt curiously at home.

A piano she was led past had its surface cluttered with photographs.

'That's my son, Christopher. Ryan's father. Handsome devil, wasn't he? Do you play the piano, lass?'

'No.'

'How about chess?'

'I know how to play but I doubt I'd be up to your standard, Mr Murphy.'

'Call me Jack, for heaven's sake, girl. You make me feel old with that "Mr Murphy" nonsense.'

Holly smiled agreement but her attention had been caught by another photograph. 'Is that Ryan?'

'Oh, don't get him started.' Ryan had been right behind his grandfather. 'Pop's opinion of the gear we use for fencing is not exactly complimentary.'

'Well, look at him,' Jack snorted. 'All done up in skin-tight, fancy silver stuff. It's girly, that's what I say.'

Holly *had* been looking at him. Couldn't look away, in fact. The action photograph could have been anyone, with the face covered by a protective mask, heavy gloves on the hands and a thick chest covering of some sort. But Jack was right. The silver trousers were quite tight. Tight enough to see the definition of calf muscles as the figure lunged, one arm wielding a wicked-looking sword, the other held high in the air. Knowing it was Ryan was disconcerting. Had Holly seen the picture somewhere else, it would have occurred to her that the figure looked something like a medieval knight who had jumped off his horse for a jousting match. She would also have conceded that the action, quite apart from the strength and grace clearly being displayed, was astonishingly sexy.

The shaft of what was these days a very unfamiliar sensation caught Holly totally by surprise and she groaned inwardly as she followed the two men into their kitchen. Along with the more platonic feelings for Ryan that were in that roller-coaster carriage, she now had to shovel in a disturbingly large quantity of sexual attraction.

But at least that disturbing element of the evening had worn off by the time they sat down to eat and Jack was telling Ryan to stop interfering, he could carve the lamb himself, thank you very much.

'Thinks he's got the monopoly on using sharp things,'

he complained to Holly. 'Probably just as well he's going to see what it's like on the other side of the fence soon. Be the first time he's had a real operation.'

'Does it bother you, Jack?'

'As if my opinion counted,' Jack huffed. But his expression, as he eased a generous slice of meat onto Ryan's plate, was one of pride. Then he winked at Holly. 'Who needs two kidneys? That's what I say. Only got one myself.'

'Really?'

'War wound.' Jack nodded. 'Caught a bullet that went straight into my left kidney. Hasn't done me any harm. Look at me. I'm ninety-six and I've still got my own teeth.'

Holly laughed but then Jack surprised her by leaning across the table and patting her hand.

'I'm delighted that Ryan's doing this. He's a good lad.'

'He is,' Holly agreed solemnly.

With that agreement, Holly found herself caught up in the bond that existed between Jack and Ryan. So much so that when she refused dessert she wasn't embarrassed that Ryan started to explain why she had to be so careful with her diet.

'Of course, if Holly comes to stay with us after discharge, you could do her one of those nice custardy things.'

'*Crème brûlée*,' Jack corrected, but his attention was on Holly again. 'You coming to stay?'

'Holly's family's in Australia,' Ryan said, before she had time to say anything. 'I thought she could put up with your war stories for a few days while she's recuperating.'

Jack chuckled. 'Just wait till they hear about this at the Returned Servicemen's Association. Someone my age running a nursing home!'

'I wouldn't expect you to look after me, Jack.' Now Holly

was embarrassed and her blush deepened as she realised the tacit acceptance of the invitation her words had implied.

'Nonsense.' The direct look Holly received from the old man held a wealth of understanding. 'I *want* to look after you, lass.' There was a distinct twinkle in the faded hazel eyes. 'You're getting a kidney that's got some of my genes in it. I say that makes you one of the family.'

'Your grandad's an absolute sweetheart,' Holly told Ryan as he drove her home.

'Yeah.' Ryan sounded wistful. 'I'll miss him when he's not around any more, that's for sure.'

'I guess every day's a bit of a bonus when you get that old.' Holly smiled as Ryan pulled into a parking slot outside her apartment block. 'I bet you'll be just like Jack when *you* hit your nineties.'

'I'll never be such a good cook.' Ryan switched off the engine and turned to watch Holly as she unclipped her safety belt. 'But I do hope I live long enough to get to know my grandchildren as well as Pop has.'

So Ryan did plan to find someone to have a family with? To have children and grandchildren?

'You've got the genes anyway,' Holly said lightly. 'You'll make it.'

Ryan's soft words were unexpected. 'You're going to have some of those genes soon, too,' he said. 'We'll both make it.'

Holly had been reaching for the doorhandle but her hand dropped back into her lap of its own accord. 'If I do, it'll be thanks to you. There's no way I can ever say thank you properly, is there?'

'You don't have to.'

Was it a trick of the yellowish light from the overhead

streetlamp struggling to get through the curtain of rain or was Ryan's gaze riveted on her mouth? For a moment, Holly could swear that Ryan intended to kiss her.

And… Oh, *God*! She *wanted* Ryan to kiss her.

She had never wanted anything so badly.

The sound of rain on the car's roof filled a silence that was measured by a heartbeat. And then another.

'Would you do this for someone else, Ryan?'

His eyebrows shot up. 'Who did you have in mind?'

The humour had always been readily available, hadn't it? Was it, in fact, a cover for something else that Holly had never recognised?

'There's hundreds of people out there who are desperate for kidneys. Steve Mersey, for instance.'

'No. I couldn't do this for a stranger.'

'What about someone you know, then? At work, say. Someone like Sue?'

Ryan hesitated for a long moment. 'No,' he said finally. He cleared his throat. 'I doubt that it would have entered my mind seriously if it hadn't been you that needed the kidney, Holly.' Another tiny pause. 'You're "it."'

Like a game of tag. Or hide and seek.

But Holly had no desire to run. Or hide.

What she desperately wanted to do was to ask why, but her mouth went dry as she saw what appeared to be an answer in Ryan's eyes.

Any rational thought that the emotional turmoil Holly was experiencing had created temporary insanity as far as Ryan was concerned was forgotten. The very real possibility that he could be sharing some of those feelings was suddenly the most exciting thing that had ever happened to Holly.

Even more exciting than being offered the possibility of a normal life through a transplant.

Holly's heart thumped painfully but any other muscles froze. She couldn't talk. Couldn't look away from Ryan. Couldn't *move*.

He could. Very slowly and with infinite tenderness, he leaned over and touched Holly's lips with his own.

Just once.

Just briefly.

But it was enough to confirm what Holly thought she might have seen in that gaze.

A reflection of how she felt about Ryan.

Nothing needed to be said. This was hardly the time or the place. The moment after that soft kiss could have been awkward but the familiar way Ryan's mouth curved into that lovely smile made everything seem perfectly fine.

'Here's to being ninety,' he said.

And Holly smiled back. 'Bring it on!'

CHAPTER SIX

FROM now on, yellow was going to be her favourite colour.

Anything golden would be welcome in Holly's life. Like the daffodils more than one person had brought to brighten her hospital room. And those flecks in Ryan Murphy's hazel eyes which were like tiny nuggets of gold. And…Holly blinked herself more properly awake and rolled cautiously onto her side to peer over the edge of her bed.

Yes!

The soft plastic bag suspended from the rail had at least three hundred mils of clear, beautiful, golden fluid inside it. Urine from a brand-new kidney that was already functioning as close to perfectly as anyone could have hoped. The catheter was due to come out the next day and Holly would miss the reassurance that bag had provided ever since she had come round from her anaesthetic to find it already beginning to fill.

'Beats watching paint dry, huh?'

'Ooh!' Startled by the voice of the visitor Holly had not heard enter her room, she moved a little too fast to raise her head back to her pillow. An expression of pain was quickly replaced by a frown of concern.

'Ryan! Are you supposed to be walking round by yourself?'

'Someone nicked my wheelchair. Besides, I needed to break out.' He was wearing a tartan dressing-gown over pyjamas and he moved carefully as he came closer, walking slowly with a slight tilt to one side. 'Might sit down for a minute now, if that's OK.'

'I think you'd better.' Holly could see a faint sheen of perspiration on Ryan's forehead and he looked pale. 'Are you all right?'

'I'm fine.' It was just as well Holly was so used to picking up when he smiled beneath a mask. Every visitor to her room had to wear one at present because the anti-rejection medication she was taking made her more susceptible to infection and that was a complication nobody wanted to see her have to deal with. Even the daffodils in her room were encased in plastic bags.

'I just had my first shower,' Ryan told her. 'It was brilliant.'

He was certainly recovering at an impressive rate. And a little colour was creeping back into his cheeks now that he was resting so Holly felt her anxiety lessen. She hadn't seen him at all on the actual day of the transplant but the nursing staff had delighted in taking dictation and delivering messages between their rooms. Yesterday Ryan had appeared in a wheelchair and now, only forty-eight hours after surgery, he was on his feet and moving independently.

'So how are *you* doing?' Ryan asked.

'I feel fantastic. I've just had a lovely nap.'

'You mean you haven't been lying here since lunch watching yourself produce urine?'

Holly just smiled. Ryan had been just as delighted as she had been when he'd spotted the catheter bag's contents yesterday. The next visitor to Holly's room was obviously amused to find both Ryan and Holly admiring the evidence of the new kidney's function.

'And I thought only us renal chaps took that much interest in that yellow stuff.'

'Hi, Ken.'

'This is just a flying visit. How are you feeling?'

'Amazingly good. I'm a bit sore and tired but I don't feel sick. I can't wait to get out of bed.'

'Tomorrow,' the surgeon promised. 'If you keep up such good results.' He tilted Holly's chart and nodded in satisfaction at the steady lines joining her vital sign measurements. 'I won't see you in the morning, though. We've got an unexpectedly big day coming up.'

'Another transplant?' Ryan queried.

'Two, in fact.' Ken dropped the chart and rested an elbow beside its clip, clearly keen to take a moment and chat to a colleague. 'Big MVA at the weekend left a seventeen-year-old girl with critical head injuries. She's been pronounced brain dead and the parents have agreed to organ donation as long as the rest of the family gets a chance to come in and say goodbye this evening.'

'Good for them,' Ryan said quietly. 'That can't have been an easy decision.'

'The liver's going to be sent to Wellington,' Ken said, 'but we've hit the jackpot with two close matches for kidneys. The heart's staying here as well. In fact, you two probably know the intended recipient.'

Holly got another nasty twinge in her abdomen as excitement made her sit up straighter. 'Michaela? Is *she* getting the heart transplant?'

'Is that a twelve-year-old girl with cardiomyopathy?'

'*Yes!*' Both Holly and Ryan spoke at the same time with

exactly the same tone of eagerness. Then they looked at each other and Holly could see the same kind of joy that had shone from Ryan's face after the successful delivery of Leo's little sister. The same kind of joy he had transmitted only yesterday when he had been wheeled to her room to say hello in person.

And Holly loved it that Ryan could be so happy for other people. She couldn't stop smiling at him. Couldn't stop the tears that pricked at the corners of her eyes. When he reached out, took hold of her hand and squeezed it, she squeezed right back.

'Ahem!' Ken sounded vaguely embarrassed. 'I'll leave you two to celebrate, then. Keep up the good recovery work, Holly. You can see how you go on your feet and I'll check in later tomorrow.'

'Thanks, Ken. Oh, do you know when Michaela's surgery is scheduled?'

'We're all kicking off about 7 a.m. One theatre will be used for the harvest surgery and the two adjoining suites will be used for the transplants. One for the heart and the other for both my kidneys.' Ken grinned. 'Sounds good, doesn't it?'

It sure sounded good to Holly.

'Theatre's not far from here,' Ryan said thoughtfully when Ken had left. 'If I can walk that far, I might go and watch. That way I could keep you posted on progress.'

'Oh, please, do.' Holly hadn't let go of Ryan's hand but he was still holding hers just as tightly.

A nurse entered the room at that moment because Holly was due for another set of recordings of her blood pressure, heart and respiration rates, temperature and urine output. Ryan left, but the magic of his touch remained long after his visit.

No matter what the future held, Holly knew that she would never feel the kind of connection with anyone else that she did with Ryan. It wasn't going to go away. She would have loved him even if she'd been a perfectly healthy bystander watching him go through this for someone else.

The fact that *his* kidney was now inside her and providing the promise of a new life was just an extra dimension. A very powerful one, admittedly, but if the unspoken attraction between them came to nothing Holly would still never have another day in her life when she didn't think of Ryan with gratitude.

And love.

Holly got out of bed the next day and was sitting on a chair after managing a tentative walk when Ryan came to tell her that Michaela was nearly out of Theatre.

'It's the most astonishing surgery, isn't it?'

Holly knew exactly what he meant. Having observed a cardiac transplant, she had seriously considered steering her career towards transplant surgery. There was a distinct moment—when the recipient's heart had been lifted clear of the chest cavity and before the donor heart filled the space—when it looked as though what the surgical team was trying to accomplish was totally beyond the realms of possibility.

'It is amazing,' she agreed readily. 'You've got someone lying there with no heart. And then you can replace it and bring them back to life. Magic.'

'It was a perfect-sized organ,' Ryan continued happily. 'The pulmonary arteries and aortic openings fitted together as though they'd never been separated.'

'Did they need to defibrillate to kick-start it?'

'Almost. It was fibrillating when the cross-clamp came off.

They'd charged up the internal paddles but gave it another thirty seconds or so and, bingo! Straight into sinus rhythm!'

'How's she looking now?'

'They were still closing when I left. I thought you might be getting impatient for news.'

'I was.'

'She was haemodynamically stable, anyway.'

'That's fantastic. I can't wait to visit.'

'She'll be in isolation for a while when she gets out of Intensive Care.'

'I know. I doubt that I could walk that far just yet anyway.'

Ryan's face softened into an encouraging smile. 'It won't be long. You're doing so well, Holly. We're all proud of you.'

Ryan was allowed home only a day later but he came to visit Holly every day and on the third visit he brought his grandfather with him.

'You're looking wonderful, lass.'

'I'm starting to look like a puffer fish thanks to the medications I'm on—but I *feel* wonderful. Better than I have for years.'

'When are they going to let you come home?'

'Soon, I hope.'

'Might be quicker,' Ryan suggested, 'if you let them know you're going to be well taken care of.'

'I don't want to impose on either of you.'

'Nonsense,' Jack said dismissively. 'We've got your room ready, lass. In my half of the house.' He winked at Holly. 'I know what the gossip can be like in these places.'

Ryan's gaze was disconcertingly steady as he listened to the exchange. He didn't care what anybody might say. Something in his expression even suggested that he might be inclined to give people rather a lot more to discuss.

Holly took a swift, inward breath. 'Well, if you're sure that it won't be a problem?'

'Why don't you make a list of any extra stuff you might need?' Ryan said calmly. 'And give us a key to your apartment.'

The notion of Ryan searching for and packing such items as clean underwear might have been enough to make Holly change her mind, but the arrival of Sue to join her other visitors provided a solution.

'I'll pack for her,' Sue declared on hearing the proposal. She beamed at Ryan and Jack. 'This is great. I've been worried about Holly trying to cope by herself but my house is total chaos thanks to my kids.'

'It makes perfect sense.' Jack nodded. 'Keep these kidneys in the family, that's what I say.'

Holly ignored in the look Sue flashed in her direction. Her friend would learn of any developments in her relationship with her boss in good time. She got the message with gratifying speed. She turned to Ryan and changed the subject.

'Grace is finally out of ICU and back on the ward. Colin said he'd call in and give you an update later. Is it true you're planning to come back to work next week?'

'I won't be in Theatre for a while yet but I feel quite well enough to manage a quiet ward round and maybe a clinic or two.'

'Cool. You won't mind if I put your name down for the fun run, then. You seemed to have forgotten to get around to it. Or do you want to give it a miss this year?'

'No way. Wouldn't miss it for the world,' Ryan said dryly.

'Will you be OK by then?'

'It's, what, at least eight weeks away? Shouldn't be a problem.'

'I'm going as Snow White,' Sue told them. 'I'm going to borrow my kids' friends to help make up the dwarf numbers. The ward's doing a *Lion King* theme, I think. African animals, anyway.'

'Great. Maybe I can be a hyena. Anything's got to be an improvement on last year's clown.'

'Sounds fun,' Holly said wistfully. 'Maybe I could do it this time.'

Everybody looked shocked. Ryan shook his head. 'Not this time, Holly. Your body's got quite enough to get used to in the next few months.'

'One step at a time,' Jack added firmly. 'Let's get you walking before you start trying to run, lass.'

Holly walked a little more each day.

Released from hospital after ten days, she spent the next eight days living in Jack's half of the old, divided villa. Her room had a very comfortable bed and an *en suite* bathroom. Ryan had even made the library visit Holly had ended up not finding time for prior to her hospitalisation, and some helpful librarian had chosen a stack of historical romances for her to sample.

It didn't matter that the worst of the winter weather had arrived and it was too nasty to set foot in the spacious garden. Jack had a fire going by the time Holly got up each day and he took as much pleasure in seeing her curled up on the sofa with her nose buried in a novel as he did in cooking small and tempting meals.

'Let's see if we can't get a bit of meat on those bones,' he said.

Ryan spent more and more of his time at the hospital so Holly only really saw him in the evenings. The first outpatient clinic he ran that week gave them plenty of dinner-time conversation on the night Jack had gone to his regular Returned Servicemen's Association meeting.

'Daniel's fighting fit and ready to try out for the school rugby team.'

'Did he get to that Blues game?'

'Sure did. Apparently, they flashed up a message on the big screen at half-time that said HI, DANIEL, HOPE YOU'RE FEELING BETTER.'

'He must have been rapt.'

'He was. I'll tell you who else is really happy and that's Callum's mum. He's into everything at play centre now and can last the whole session without any symptoms.'

'Has Leo been back for his post-op check yet?'

'No, but I heard his little sister is home now. She's put on enough weight and she's not showing any after-effects from her unconventional entrance to the world.'

'Did they decide on a name?'

'Sophie.'

'Oh, nice. And what about Michaela? Is she still doing well?'

'They're talking about letting her go home this week.'

'Fantastic. And Grace? How was she today? Have the antibiotics kicked in yet for that chest infection?'

'Seem to have. Hopefully she won't get any more setbacks.'

'I miss them all,' Holly said. 'I've never had this long away from work at a stretch, which seems ironic because I feel better than I ever have.'

'Doug won't let you back on deck for another week—wasn't that what he told you at your check-up yesterday?'

'Yes, but—'

'But you're getting cabin fever stuck in the house.'

'I'd love to get out for a good long walk. I wish it would stop raining.'

'I can make it stop,' Ryan said.

'Oh, yeah?' The face Holly pulled made her realise just how comfortable she was in Ryan's company now. There was an easy familiarity between them. And more…. The sense of relaxation lessened considerably as Holly experienced another twinge of the physical attraction that still showed no signs of weakening.

Maybe Ryan was feeling it as well. Holly may have been resting and recuperating for the last few days but there was a definite sense of waiting for more than physical recovery, and surely that wouldn't be hanging in the air so strongly if it was purely one-sided. Holly wasn't going to push any boundaries, however. If it was going to happen, it would happen in its own good time.

And maybe sooner than she'd anticipated.

'So, just how are you going to make it stop raining, Ryan?'

'I'll show you.' He stood up, went to the briefcase lying under a soggy raincoat and snapped it open to remove an envelope. He waved it at Holly. 'Tickets,' he said triumphantly. 'Two rooms for four days at the Kula Island resort on the Coral Coast in Fiji.'

'What *are* you talking about?'

'I thought we both deserved a treat before we went back to work properly. A few days of real rest. Sun and total relaxation. A final boost for recuperation. What do you say, Holly?'

Ryan was looking curiously intense and Holly knew why. He was offering more than a holiday here. If Holly agreed to go away with him, she would be giving him a very clear message that she was willing to take their relationship to a completely new level.

And she *was* willing. But…

'I can't go out of the country, Ryan. Not right now.'

'Why not?'

'What if I had an episode of rejection or something?'

'I talked to Doug about that. I'll carry whatever supplies we could need in the way of monitoring gear and anti-rejection drugs we might need to juggle. We're both doctors, Holly. We're both capable of recognising any kind of complication early enough to deal with it. And Fiji's only a four-hour flight away. It's hardly the back of beyond.'

Holly wasn't annoyed that Ryan had been talking to her renal physician behind her back again. How could she be? After so many days of being confined by relentlessly wet weather on top of a stretch of being institutionalised, he was offering her a taste of paradise.

'I've never been to Fiji. I haven't even been near a beach properly in years.'

'I know. I remember you telling Ken that when he said he'd take care that your scar wasn't too obvious when you were wearing a bikini.'

'And so you thought of this? A beach trip in the middle of winter? That's so sweet.'

'So…' Ryan's eyes looked much darker than normal and his face was very serious. 'Will you trust me to look after you? Shall we go and enjoy some sunshine together?'

And would that be all they enjoyed together? Holly knew her expression was probably as serious as Ryan's. Her voice actually wobbled a little when she spoke.

'I'd love to, Ryan. I really would.'

* * *

It was bliss.

Away from the winter rain. Away from any reminders of work or study and an ideal excuse to postpone having to think about returning to that lonely apartment. With the prospect of nothing to do other than rest, choose from a glorious array of fresh tropical fruit and seafood, swim and bask in the sun or wander through the maze of tracks on the resort island that led to everything from rock pools on the beach to deep tropical forest.

Holly slept for most of the early morning flight to Fiji and slept again after the boat transfer to the island and lunch in the shade of coconut palms by an invitingly clear blue swimming pool.

Ryan's tap on her door at around 4 p.m. woke her. He came in, armed with a blood-pressure cuff, stethoscope and thermometer.

'House call,' he announced.

The bed Holly was still lying on dipped as Ryan sat on the side. 'I don't usually make house calls,' he informed her. 'I'll have to send the bill later.' He pointed the thermometer at Holly's mouth. 'Open wide.'

He noted down all his recordings in a small notebook. 'Everything's fine,' he pronounced, 'though your heart rate's up a bit. Almost tachycardic, in fact. How are you feeling?'

'I feel fine.' Holly felt her cheeks reddening. She knew why her heart rate was elevated. Here she was, lounging on her bed after a nap, wearing only a camisole top and shorts. From her window she could see the exciting vista of a tropical paradise begging to be explored. A place she had never been to before.

And much closer to hand was a man she was finding

even more exciting to be near. How could she have ever thought that Ryan's slightly disreputable, shaggy hair and those strong, craggy features prevented him from being considered conventionally good-looking? He was gorgeous. Eyes that shone with warmth and a quiet appreciation of the good things that life—and other people—had to offer. Lips that she knew were as soft as they looked thanks to that brief kiss that seemed a lifetime ago. And that smile… That slow curve that deepened the lines defining his cheeks and made his eyes crinkle at the corners.

The surgeon's hands with that sure touch from artistically long fingers. Fingers that had just been touching her body as they'd rested on her wrist to find her traitorous heart making the fact of her attraction to him only too obvious. But she wasn't alone in that, was she? Holly could see the faint pulse of Ryan's carotid artery on the side of his neck and with a smile she caught his wrist and laid her fingers on his skin.

'At least a hundred beats per minute,' she said softly. 'How are *you* feeling?'

Instead of the expected brisk dismissal of any possible physical discomfort, Ryan gave a soft groan as his gaze locked with Holly's.

'I'm afraid I'm feeling very, very attracted to you, Holly Williams. That's the only reason I'm tachycardic.'

And here was the moment Holly had been waiting for. The opportunity to admit what they both knew was simmering between them. Time to throw that door into a new future wide open. It took only a single, whispered word from Holly.

'Same.'

The stethoscope Ryan had still been holding slipped from his hand unnoticed as he bent to kiss Holly. He touched her lips with the same kind of tenderness she remembered from that first kiss and it was just as brief. For a heart-stopping moment, she thought that was as far as he intended to go. Did he think she was still too physically fragile for this? With a touch of something close to panic, she slid her hands over his shoulders to encourage him to stay close.

But he had only drawn back far enough to search her face for an instant, and whatever he saw in her eyes was enough to elicit another groan. Not one of frustration this time, however. This sound was of pure desire. And there was nothing remotely familiar about the kiss that came now. Ryan's mouth was firm beneath the softness, searching and claiming every cell of Holly's lips as he moved to lie on the bed next to her. She sighed under the delicious onslaught to her senses and with the first exquisite touch of Ryan's tongue to hers and the slide of his hand to her breast, Holly knew she was totally lost to this man.

Holly had never felt desire like this. She wanted so much she doubted she could ever have enough, but it seemed like she wouldn't get much further than the starting flags this time. Ryan pulled away again.

'Did Doug say anything to you about limitations on your physical activities?'

'I'm not to lift anything heavy for six to eight weeks but I can judge for myself how fast I increase my exercise levels.'

'Did he say anything about sex?'

Holly dropped her gaze as she reddened slightly. 'I think he said I could resume normal sexual activities in about four weeks. I didn't take much notice because my normal activities in that department have been non-existent for longer than I care to remember.'

'You want them to stay that way?'

'Are you kidding?' Holly ran her tongue slowly over her lower lip as she raised her gaze, delighting in the flare of desire she saw in Ryan's eyes.

'It hasn't been four weeks.'

'It's practically three, though,' Holly said eagerly. 'And I feel great.'

Ryan smiled. 'I could have told you that, my love.' His hand was on her breast again, his thumb tracing slow circles around her nipple that sent sharp spirals of sensation straight to the depths of Holly's abdomen.

His hand moved, tracing her ribs and then resting gently over the scar from her surgery. 'Great isn't quite the word I'd have picked, however. You're sensational, Holly. I just can't believe the way touching you makes me feel.' He slid both hands to cup her bottom, pulling the length of her body closer to his own.

'Maybe,' he said softly, 'if we were very, very careful and I was very gentle, we could see just how far we could get.'

'Mmm.' Holly intended to make sure they got to the very end of that particular track.

'But not right now.' Ryan sighed deeply and his hold gentled so that Holly was lying in his arms, simply being hugged. The disappointment was startlingly intense.

'Why not?'

'Because I haven't got a condom,' he said sadly.

'We've both had every blood test known to man to check for any communicable diseases. I doubt there's a couple anywhere on earth who could start a relationship with the clean bill of health we've got.'

'I'm not talking STDs. There's no way on earth I'd risk your health by playing Russian roulette in the pregnancy stakes.'

'Oh…' Had she been too blinded by desire to think of that or was there something subconscious going on that made the idea of having Ryan's baby attractive enough to not want to be bothered with preventative measures? But he was right, of course. While kidney transplant patients were quite capable of a successful pregnancy, they were advised to wait at least two years before conception. And it was ridiculous to be even thinking of it at this stage of their relationship, wasn't it? How could she possibly be so sure that Ryan was 'the one'?

'How about a walk on the beach instead?' he asked. 'We could find somewhere to sit and watch the sunset.'

'Do you think there's a chemist's shop somewhere on this island?'

'People come here to play,' Ryan said confidently. 'Sun, sand, surf and sex. Of course there's a chemist's shop.' He kissed Holly again. 'Good things are worth waiting for. And what we're going to wait for is going to be a lot better than good.'

It was.

Better than good. Better than fantastic. It was stunning.

Love-making that was slow and careful, which had the effect of making it almost unbearably intense.

And, on a completely different level, it was equally magical to sleep in Ryan's arms and to wake with that warmth and comfort of having someone to share every part of her day. Surely no new lovers had ever felt quite this close. This connected. Ryan touched the healing scar on Holly's belly that first morning they woke together.

'I love that it's my kidney in there,' he told her solemnly. 'I wanted to do this for you so badly.'

'Because you weren't able to help your wife? Elise?'

'No. Don't ever think that, Holly. You're nothing at all like Elise and the way I feel about you is just as different. I love you. More than I ever thought it was possible to love anyone.'

The words sent a thrill right down Holly's spine.

'I love you, too,' she whispered. 'I think I have for a long time but I didn't let myself recognise it. There's been no space in my life for any kind of relationship for so long.'

'Same,' Ryan said. 'But I'm making space from now on.'

'Me, too.'

'How much space, Holly?'

'As much as you want.'

'Are you sure? Because I want it all. I want to live with you. To spend as much of every day as I can showing you how much I love you. I…I want to marry you, Holly.'

Holly couldn't say anything in response for a moment. Her brain was whirling. To spend the rest of her life with Ryan. Could she trust that the overwhelming feelings she had for him were not simply a byproduct of the experience they had both just been through? That they wouldn't fade when life settled into a new normality? To never have to go back to that apartment and be alone again held so much appeal it was enough to sound a warning. That apartment had been reality for a long time. She was in a place with Ryan right now that was so far removed from reality that what happened here might not last on their return.

But it was too hard to try and think rationally. The best Holly could manage was to sound a note of caution.

'Let's take it one step at a time,' she said finally. 'Jack said it the other day, didn't he? We need to walk before we run.'

That first step was another three days in paradise.

Each day, Holly felt noticeably stronger and there were

no signs that her body had any intention of rejecting Ryan's gift. He checked carefully at least twice a day.

'Your blood pressure is fine and your temperature's normal. Any abdominal pain?'

'Less every day.'

'Any pain on passing urine?'

'No.'

'Frequency?'

'No.'

'Any ankle swelling? Feeling breathless?'

'No. I feel so good, Ryan. I want to go swimming today and then see if I can walk up to the top of that hill behind the golf course.'

'A swim's a good idea. Pool or ocean?'

'Oh, ocean, definitely. And let's get a couple of those deck chairs and find a place to sunbathe.'

'You'll have to be careful with sun exposure. You're going to burn a lot more easily with the medications you're on. Have you taken your pills this morning?'

'Yes, sir! And I've got a bucket of SPF 45 sunscreen.' Holly's smile was mischievous. As much as she loved having Ryan so concerned for her welfare, she felt nothing like an invalid any more. She wanted to enjoy every remaining moment they had on this island. 'Want to help me put that sunscreen on?'

'Try and stop me.'

They swam in water warm enough to be a caress and clear enough to watch the tiny jewel-like fish that darted beneath the surface.

They walked through gardens and forests, stopping to

sniff the fragrance of tropical flowers like frangipani and admire the astonishing variety of orchids.

They watched for, and delighted in, the colourful, parrot-like birds the island had been named for and the pre-historic-looking iguanas that clung to branches by curling long, spindly toes.

They held hands and sat to listen to the sounds of the island. The gentle wash of surf, the songs of the islanders and the distant laughter of children.

They ate fresh, sun-ripened fruits like mangoes, pine-apples, papayas and guava, and tasted local fish and even octopus.

They slept.

And made love.

And they didn't want to go home.

Four days had been a blink in their lifetimes but the brief gap from normality had marked such a change there was no going back.

Holly had to trust that this would last. She wasn't single any more. She was part of a couple and she was happier— and healthier—than she could ever remember being.

Life just couldn't get any better than this, could it?

CHAPTER SEVEN

A NEW life.

Anchored in the familiarity of the old but so different that Holly felt she had moved from living in a black and white movie to one of glorious Technicolor.

The hospital was the same. A new series of patients came to replace the recent ones, as always, and Bella was one of the first. The surgery to correct her heart problem was straightforward and Holly was relieved to learn from Bella's parents that any practice of veterinary skills on their puppy usually amounted to a game of tug-of-war with an old bandage after an unsuccessful attempt to wrap some part of its anatomy.

And, as always, the outpatient clinics provided a thread of continuity that Holly loved. She delighted in seeing the rapid progress towards normal childhoods that little Callum and Leo and now even baby Grace were making. She visited Michaela the day after she returned from Fiji, which was the day before Michaela would be allowed home to begin *her* new life.

'You're going to feel like a brand-new person,' Holly told her, with a hug. 'You're going to love every minute of it.'

Like Holly did. The physical well-being that had her

wide awake early in the morning, coping with long days of sessions in Theatre, outpatient clinics, ward rounds and meetings would have been enough to transform her life over the next few weeks all by itself, but that felt like only a small part of her new world.

Her apartment was basically still the same. The wealth of paraphernalia required for home dialysis had gone from the bedroom, however, and most of the clothes had been gradually moved from the wardrobe and chest of drawers because Holly had not returned to her old home to stay after the trip away with Ryan.

She wasn't quite sure how she had moved into his half of the old villa without it seeming like another major life change. It had just happened. The flight back from Fiji had arrived late in Auckland so it had been sensible to go back to the Murphys' where Jack had had supper waiting for them.

If Ryan's grandfather had been surprised when he'd seen Holly the next morning after Ryan had said casually that she wouldn't be needing her room in Jack's half of the house that night, he'd given no sign of it. He waited a week to say anything at all, despite it being so obvious that Ryan and Holly were in love with each other, and even then his comment was matter-of-fact.

'She's part of the family, anyway, with that kidney. It was meant to be, that's what I say.'

It certainly felt as though it was meant to be. And it was all so easy. Nights in Ryan's arms only increased their magic as they both gained physical strength, and on the nights they didn't indulge in love-making, Holly would still not have wanted to be anywhere else in the world.

'Marry me,' Ryan urged. 'Sell the apartment.'

'Soon,' Holly promised. 'I want to get used to things first. Doesn't it sometimes all seem a bit too good to be true?'

'No.' He pulled Holly into his arms. 'It just seems perfect. I love you, Holly Williams. And I want to take care of you. For ever.'

And maybe that was enough to make Holly procrastinate about taking steps to formalise their commitment. Her apartment had always been a symbol of her independence. Her ability to take care of herself. Yes, she wanted a relationship with Ryan. Marriage and a family. But it had to be on equal terms, and while any misgivings could be put down to not knowing each other well enough yet, Holly was still reluctant to go public by announcing an engagement or plans for marriage. Those tiny doubts would need to be put to rest first.

In the early days after her transplant, Ryan's attention to monitoring her physical condition and watching for any signs of rejection had been welcome. Reassuring. As the weeks passed and Holly's drug regime was reduced to a level that removed most of the side effects and the extra weight she had gained without putting her into rejection, his level of concern became less welcome.

'Taken your pills?'

'Yes, Ryan.' Holly finally rebelled on the day that marked a month's anniversary of her moving in with Ryan. 'Please, don't ask me that every morning.'

'I'm only trying to help.'

'It's not something I'm going to forget. I've been taking pills for years without needing supervision.'

'Am I not allowed to show an interest in your state of health, then?'

'Of course you are.' Holly felt churlish for being annoyed. 'But it *is* a state of health now, Ryan. I'm not sick any more.'

Thanks to him, she had to add silently, which had the effect of making her feel even more guilty at having caused the bewildered expression on his face.

'And I only have to take a couple of pills now. I used to take handfuls. This is nothing.'

'Which would make it easier to forget, wouldn't it?'

'Fair enough.' Holly didn't like the frisson of tension between them. And how ridiculous to allow that tension to remain when it was there because he cared so much about her. At least he'd stopped taking her blood pressure every day. He didn't even get offended when Holly refused to let him take it on a weekly basis.

'I have regular check-ups with Doug,' she reminded him. 'I'm not living with you in order to have a personal physician on hand.'

'Fair enough. But you'll tell me, won't you, if you're not feeling well?'

'You'll be the first to know,' Holly promised.

'I am glad you're doing so well, darling. It's wonderful to see you looking so much more alive at the end of a day. Even coping with nights on call.'

'I feel so much more alive. I'm going to get back into a real exercise programme now. It's getting light enough in the mornings to get a good walk in before work and I'm thinking of joining that gym that's so close to St Margaret's.'

'A walk's a great idea. I'll come with you. I've got to start getting into shape for that fun run.'

'Have you decided on a costume?'

'Yeah. I'm going as a lion.'

'Excellent choice.' Holly reached up to ruffle his shaggy hair. 'You've got the mane for it already.'

Ryan managed a convincingly leonine growl as he wrapped his arms around Holly, lifting her off her feet and scraping his teeth on her neck as she gave a co-operatively frightened squeak. Then he set her down and their smiles faded under the intensity of the glance they shared.

'I love you, Holly.'

'I love you, too, Ryan.'

The suburban streets undulated gently and provided perfect routes for gradually building up stamina. Ryan got up early with Holly each day and accompanied her, using the stretch of beach nearby and the biggest inclines to jog and sprint instead of walk. When Holly started jogging to keep up one day, however, Ryan immediately slowed his pace.

'Hey, take it easy,' he admonished. 'You're not ready to train for a marathon yet.'

No. But Holly felt she was more than ready to train for a fun run that was still over three weeks away. Even if she couldn't complete it, she wanted to take part. Everybody at work, including her patients' families, was taking such pleasure in her recovery from such a long, debilitating illness. The sponsorship Holly could gather for joining the run properly could be enormous. People would be far too used to her being healthy by this time next year and the same support might not be there. And she could manage it, she knew she could. Holly was itching to start really pushing her boundaries now. In every direction.

When an urgent summons to the emergency department interrupted their ward round that morning, Holly ran ahead of Ryan and only heeded his admonition to slow down when they reached the stairs.

'Did they say what this boy has been impaled *with*?'

'He was standing on a large tree branch when it broke. He fell along with it and got impaled on a smaller branch.'

'And it's a chest injury?'

'Entry wound is in the abdomen with probable splenic injury, but it's angled up and Tania sounded fairly confident that there may be cardiac involvement.'

Emergency cardiac surgery on children following trauma was unusual enough to get the adrenaline flowing and the tension ratcheted up several notches as they entered the strained atmosphere in the resuscitation area of Emergency.

'Please,' a woman cried. 'Just take it *out*!'

'We can't do that, Mrs Johnson. It could make the injury a great deal worse. Taylor will have to go to Theatre to have the stick removed. Our cardiac surgeon is on his way. Here he is now, in fact.' ED consultant Tania Townsend looked relieved at Ryan's arrival. 'Ryan, this is Jane Johnson—Taylor's mother.'

The woman actually reached out to grab Ryan's hand. 'Please, you have to help my son. He's—'

'I know,' Ryan interrupted. He paused for only a few moments to reassure the distraught woman and then they were beside the small, still figure lying on the bed.

'Taylor is nine years old,' Tania informed them. 'He was conscious when the paramedics arrived and they stabilised the stick and transported him straight away. It's now…' she glanced up at the clock '…thirty five minutes since injury.'

'You've got a chest drain in,' Ryan observed. 'Haemothorax?'

'Haemopneumothorax,' the consultant reported. 'He was in severe respiratory distress by the time we got him. Initial drainage of blood was 1100 mils and it's still draining at a rate that suggests active bleeding in the chest. I'd put him in Class III shock. He had a litre of saline *en route* and we've established another wide-bore line and run in a second litre. We've got cross-matched blood running now and should get some type-specific through by the time you get to Theatre. Vital signs improved initially but they're dropping again. Systolic pressure's currently 75.'

'Chest X-ray?'

'Here. Before and after the insertion of the chest drain.' Tania was pointing to the illuminated screens. 'There's some rib fractures and still enough blood in the chest cavity to obscure things.'

'Doesn't look like he's got a cardiac tamponade,' Ryan noted, 'but that stick's got to be just about touching the heart.'

'It is,' Holly put in. 'Come and look at this, Ryan.'

Holly was beside the bed and had crouched so that the stick protruding from the boy's upper abdomen was at eye level. It moved up and down in time with the respirations now being provided by the ventilator, but Holly had spotted a more subtle movement. One that was in synch with the spikes on the ECG monitor.

'Good grief,' Ryan murmured. 'It must be actually in contact with the heart.'

'Theatre's on standby,' Tania told them. 'I alerted them at the same time I called you.'

'General surgery?'

'They'll meet you up there.'

Their patient would need a laparotomy as well as a thoracotomy thanks to the abdominal injury that was no doubt contributing to the boy's dangerous level of blood loss. Holly knew that Theatre was going to be crowded and

until they opened this youngster's chest, they had no real
idea what kind of damage they would have to deal with.

It was going to be a battle to save young Taylor's life and
Holly was aware of a thrill of excitement as she stood beside
Ryan, scrubbing up in preparation of the emergency surgery.
She cast more than one glance at the man beside her.

If it had been *her* child waiting for a surgeon's knife in
this situation then Ryan Murphy would be her first choice.
Maybe, one day, she might have the confidence and skill
herself to face such a challenge so calmly.

Having opened the chest and retracted only one side to
avoid moving the stick, the surgeons could see nothing but
a pool of blood that shouldn't have been there.

'Suction, please,' Ryan requested. 'Has that new lot of
blood arrived yet?'

'Just,' the anaesthetist responded. 'Hanging the first unit
now.'

Holly sucked the blood clear and they could see the
other end of the small branch on the inside of the chest wall.

'It's lacerated the pericardium and the surface of the
ventricle,' Ryan announced. 'It's nicked the inferior vena
cava as well, which is where all this blood is coming from.
Suction again, Holly, thanks. And I need a clamp.'

With the bleeding from the major blood vessel leading
into the heart controlled, it was possible to remove the
short length of branch and start to clean up and repair the
damage. Miraculously, the penetrating object had stopped
just short of rupturing a chamber of the child's heart, which
would have proved rapidly fatal.

'Pressure's on its way up finally,' the anaesthetist
informed them. 'Ninety systolic.'

Taylor's spleen had been grazed by the stick but did not

require removal. With the ongoing blood loss stopped and the patient's condition improving, it was a pleasure for everybody present to watch Ryan's meticulous attention to cleaning the wound as much as possible and closing the chest again.

'He's one lucky little boy, isn't he? He's going to need a good course of antibiotics and he'll have a couple of sizeable scars, but that's about it. Keep that stick—I'm sure the family's going to want it as a souvenir.'

Holly witnessed the joy of Taylor's parents as Ryan met them afterwards to relay the good news. They were hours late finishing their ward round but neither minded a bit. Holly had never felt so inspired.

'I'm going to register to sit my Part 2 next year,' she told Ryan. 'I can't wait to become a fully qualified surgeon.'

'It's a huge amount of work. Are you sure you want to throw yourself into a study regime like that so soon?'

'I'm sure,' Holly said firmly. Ryan wasn't going to persuade her to slow down on this one. She had always been prepared to fight for what she wanted most. She'd *had* to fight for it up till now and maybe old habits never quite died. But to her pleasant surprise, Ryan didn't even try to talk her out of anything. He smiled a real Ryan smile instead.

'Then I'll do whatever I can to help you,' he said.

The realisation that she might still have to fight for some of what she wanted came a few days later after an outpatient clinic where they had seen Leo and given him an enthusiastic final clearance after his surgery. Bianca had brought the family's newest addition along to the appointment and, at six weeks old, Sophie was still tiny.

She wore a velvety soft, pink sleepsuit and when Holly held her, she smiled. Holly was smitten.

'I want one,' she confessed to Ryan as they lay in each other's arms late that night.

'So do I, my love.'

'Shall we try? After I finish my exams next year?'

'Sure. Why not? It could take a while, though. We might want to get started on the paperwork well before we set up a nursery.'

'But it might happen straight away. I wouldn't want to cope with exams *and* morning sickness.'

She felt Ryan's whole body tense. 'Morning sickness? You're not actually considering a *pregnancy*, are you?'

Holly smiled. 'That's the usual way most people have a baby.'

'You're not most people.' Ryan pushed himself away from Holly, propping himself up on one elbow so that he seemed to loom over her in the darkness. 'The risks of you having your own child are way too much, Holly.'

'But you said you wanted one, too.'

'I was talking about adoption.'

'But…' Holly felt bewildered. Adoption to her was a second choice. Acceptable, certainly, but only if it was not possible to have the child of the man she loved enough to want to spend the rest of her life with. 'But I want *your* baby, Ryan.'

She felt, rather than saw, his head shaking. 'After all you've been through, Holly, how can you even consider it? Polycystic kidney disease is an autosomal dominant inheritable disease. Any child of ours would have a fifty per cent chance of having it.'

'And of those people, half of them are going to get

through life with no symptoms. Only fifty per cent of people with PKD require dialysis treatment before they're sixty or even older.'

'That's a one in four chance of being affected, then.'

'And that wouldn't even show up until adulthood. Half a million people in the States have PKD, Ryan. There's research going on all the time. We're talking twenty years down the track. There could be all kinds of advances in both diagnosis and treatment by then.'

'It's still far too much of a risk.'

Holly was silent for a long moment. 'Yes,' she said finally. 'It *is* a risk, but think about this. My parents might not have known about that risk but even if they had I wouldn't resent them passing it on to me. I'm glad I'm alive and I'm going to fight to stay alive and as healthy as possible. Yes, I've had tough times but a lot of people can be born perfectly healthy and have it much harder than I have. And I've had my share of pure joy as well.'

She reached up and touched Ryan's face. 'I'm happier right now than anyone who has ever walked this earth. I'm *glad* I was born.'

Ryan caught her hand, held her palm against his lips and kissed it. 'Not as glad as I am, darling.'

'If you still feel this strongly about it when we're ready to start a family, I'm prepared to compromise.'

'Compromise? What—adopt half a baby?'

Holly smiled. 'No, you idiot. I'm talking about fertility treatment. Using a donor egg, perhaps, so I can still have the joy of being pregnant and giving birth to our child.'

Ryan's grip on her hand tightened. 'But the risks for that are huge, too.'

'Every pregnancy has its share of risk. To both the mother and baby.'

'Not as much as it would be in your case.'

'There are lots of success stories out there for kidney transplant women having their own babies.' Holly squeezed Ryan's hand now, hopefully reassuringly. 'I want to be one of those women, Ryan.'

He lay down again and gathered Holly into his arms, holding her tightly enough for it to be vaguely uncomfortable.

'I love you,' Ryan said almost fiercely. 'I want to keep you safe.'

'I know,' Holly whispered, 'but you can't wrap me in cotton wool, sweetheart. I want to live but I also want to get as much as I can out of every minute of being alive.'

'We'll work it out,' he said softly. 'We'll find a way through this together.' He kissed Holly. A touch of reassurance that quickly became something more.

A confirmation of their love? Or was it a distraction? A way of avoiding an issue that Holly couldn't quite put her finger on but which she knew was important.

The feeling that she was missing a hidden layer in their differing viewpoints was strong enough to linger for Holly. There was something disturbing enough about it to want to let it go but Holly knew that she couldn't afford to do that.

She knew that Ryan cared about her. He wasn't trying to undermine her autonomy or to take away her choices about what she did with her life or how she used her body. For heaven's sake, it had been Ryan who'd given her the chance to use her body in ways that would have been only a dream just a matter of weeks ago.

He loved her. He would support her choices. Just as he

intended to do regarding her career. It wouldn't be the easiest life to manage two high-powered careers and still have the time and energy to make a marriage work well, but Holly was absolutely confident that Ryan would do whatever it took.

Just as she would.

The nagging worry just wouldn't go away completely, however, and it stayed with Holly throughout the next day. By the time she reached her last task and was feeling somewhat weary, it became even more difficult not to let that worry gain precedence over what she needed to do. Seven-year-old Hannah was being admitted prior to surgery for a localised narrowing in her aorta that was preventing oxygenated blood from the heart reaching her lower body.

The condition had not been severe enough to be picked up close to birth, and other blood vessels had taken over the job of getting the blood to the right places, becoming greatly enlarged in the process. The left ventricle of the heart had also become enlarged due to the workload of getting past the obstruction but it had been a routine examination that had detected Hannah's high blood pressure and a heart murmur that had led to diagnosis.

Holly scanned Hannah's notes briefly to get her mind properly on track before going to see her patient. Drug treatment to combat the hypertension had been instigated two weeks prior to surgery and the response had been good. Hopefully, she wouldn't need any drug support once the defect in her aorta had been corrected. It was hard on young children having to take pills every day.

At least Ryan had given up those parent-like reminders to Holly about her anti-rejection medication. He could take her viewpoint on board and change his behaviour accordingly, couldn't he? And Holly could understand where *he* was coming from. Of course he had a vested interest in the performance of a body part that used to be his own. Who wouldn't?

She could understand his viewpoint about having a child of her own as well. But Ryan now trusted her to remember her pills and monitor her own health. He trusted that she could take on and cope with the long hours and study needed to pass her final exams and become a qualified surgeon. So surely he could come to trust her judgement regarding a possible pregnancy? That she could be equally responsible about any extra risks she took with her health?

Holly was confident that she could find a way to convince him. Only not right now because there were other things to think about. Like Hannah. Holly went to the single room that had been Michaela's not so long ago and found a rather frightened-looking girl with the lovely combination of red-gold hair and brown eyes who was much happier to talk about school than her medical condition.

'I love art the best,' she told Holly. 'Drawing and painting.'

'She's very good at it,' her mother said proudly. 'You're going to be famous one day, aren't you, darling?'

Hannah's smile was modest. 'I could draw something for you, if you like,' she said to Holly.

'I'd love that.'

'What would you like a picture of?'

'Oh, gosh. Anything.' Holly's gaze wandered in search of inspiration and didn't have to go far. A bright frieze decorated the room in which jungle animals peered through improbably lurid vegetation. 'A lion,' she said with conviction, 'that's what I'd like.' And that naturally reminded her of Ryan and the costume he intended to wear for the fun run. Holly pulled her gaze away from the frieze as Hannah spoke again.

'How long do I have to be in here?'

'It shouldn't be for more than a few days. I've just got to make sure you're OK for the operation first. How are you feeling?'

'OK, I guess.'

'She's been coughing a bit,' her mother said anxiously.

'Has she?' That could be a side effect from the medication to lower blood pressure but Holly made a mental note to pay particular attention to listening to Hannah's chest. An active infection would mean having to delay surgery. Checking the chart on the end of the bed revealed a normal temperature. 'Anything else? Do you have a headache, Hannah?'

'A bit.'

'Runny nose?'

'A bit.'

Holly took her time to examine Hannah carefully. There was just a suggestion that she might be coming down with a viral illness and that meant she'd have to confer with Ryan. When she left to go and phone him, Hannah's mother followed her from the room, clearly wanting to talk, so Holly stopped.

'Is she really sick, do you think?'

'I'm going to get Mr Murphy to come and see her as well. I don't think it's anything serious but he may want to leave the surgery for a day or so just to make sure.'

'Oh, no! I really wanted to get this over with. It's such a worry. It's a really big operation, isn't it?'

'Open chest surgery is never undertaken lightly,' Hannah agreed, 'but Hannah's operation is straightforward. She doesn't need to go on bypass. All we need to do is remove the narrowed section of the aorta and join it up again.'

'And that's going to cure her? She's not going to get any of those horrible complications they told us about, like heart failure and strokes?'

'Hannah's at the right age for this procedure to completely reverse her high blood pressure and remove the threat of aneurysms and heart failure. We're confident that this will be the only surgery she's going to need.'

Holly glanced through the window of the door behind them and smiled at Hannah, who was busy with a pad of paper and a packet of coloured felt pens. The girl pointed to the frieze behind her and Holly gave her a thumbs-up sign to show she understood that Hannah was already working on her lion picture.

And then, thanks to the association with lions, and in a blinding flash of inspiration, it struck her.

The fun run was three weeks away. Enough time for Holly to train and gather sponsorship. If she wore a costume that was enough of a disguise, Ryan wouldn't need to know anything about it until she crossed the finish line.

And wouldn't that make a statement about how capable she was of making her own choices and judging what she was physically able to achieve?

It could well be enough to convince Ryan and that would spell the end of that nagging worry. Holly gave a tiny, decisive nod before turning back to make sure Hannah's mother was feeling reassured.

She couldn't afford not to try, could she? She might not

be able to run the whole way but making the attempt should be enough and it didn't matter if she had to walk the last bit.

She would do it, though. One way or another, Holly was determined to reach that finish line.

CHAPTER EIGHT

MAYBE that finish line was further away than she'd thought.

Holly clung to the side bars of the machine as the belt her feet had been moving on gradually slowed. Her breath came in painful gasps and her heart pounded so hard it was alarming. Trickles of perspiration were running down her back and leg muscles shrieked a loud protest.

'How long was that?'

'Two minutes.'

'You're kidding!' Holly's face screwed into lines of dismay. She kept her head down and concentrated on getting her breath back. How could she be so unfit? She'd been walking every morning and feeling like she could easily join Ryan on his faster sections, but two minutes on the treadmill at the closest gymnasium to St Margaret's had been a revelation.

The personal trainer assigned to Holly's initial evaluation was a young and extremely fit-looking woman called Janine who was currently standing beside the treadmill with a clipboard in her hands.

'OK. You've been stopped for one minute.' She leaned in to see the reading on the display panel on the front of the treadmill. 'That's not so bad. Your heart rate is dropping quite fast. Good recovery.'

Holly could take a deeper breath now. 'I'm horribly unfit, though.'

'How long is it since you've run for that long?'

'Probably ten years.'

'Well, there you go. And you've been unwell for a long time. Plus you've had major surgery recently. You can't expect to get out and run a marathon straight away.'

'I don't want to run a marathon. I'm just aiming for a fun run. Maybe eight kilometres or so. I don't even need to run the whole way. I could walk whenever I got tired.'

'When is it?'

'Three weeks away.' The pain of this first attempt was fading. 'Do you reckon I can make it?'

Janine tried to look encouraging but doubt was written all over her face. 'How often can you get to the gym?'

'Every day,' Holly said with conviction. She'd find a way somehow. Ryan had been supportive when she had said she was going ahead with her intention to join the gym, but he thought she was planning a gradual pro- gramme of weightlifting to boost general fitness and Holly hadn't disillusioned him.

She couldn't afford to appear obsessive about attendance, though. Two or three visits a week would be the maximum number that would seem reasonable but Ryan didn't have to know about every visit, did he? Holly could slip in a session in the occasional lunch-break or use the time when Ryan made it to his regular fencing club night or embarked on a mini chess tournament with his grandfather.

Maybe it was too big an ask but there was no harm in trying. If she became unwell in some way, she would put the brakes on, but she was hoping she wouldn't have to. After that moment of inspiration the previous day, she'd rung a costume shop after making an appointment at the gym, and from the animal costumes available had chosen that of a black panther. With enough face paint on, Ryan wouldn't recognise her in a hurry and he'd be way ahead of her in the run in any case. The image of seeing his amazement—and pride—when she crossed the finish line was too good to give up.

'See?' she'd be able to say. 'I *can* do it.'

The sneaking suspicion that Ryan might be a lot less than pleased by the fact she was pushing herself so hard was easy enough to shove under a mental carpet. It was *her* body after all. *Her* choice of how hard she pushed. Holly had lived with such limitations on her physical capabilities for so long, it was a little scary to have the boundaries removed. How far could she go? It was exciting as well as scary. Holly wanted to find out just how much she *was* capable of and if she didn't give the boundaries a good shove, how would she ever know?

Holly managed two and a half minutes on the treadmill the following day before she felt like she was about to die. And three minutes the day after that, when she took an hour from her work day when Ryan was in a meeting with hospital administration staff to discuss departmental budgeting.

It was an effort to appear cheerful when she headed back to the hospital to meet Ryan and check on their patients. The goal of completing the fun run with any kind of style seemed impossible if she could only gain a half a minute a day. Perhaps she should just give up and go back to the gentle kind of programme that everybody thought more suitable for a recent kidney transplant patient. Ryan's surprise and a confidence that she could make her own decisions regarding her body might just have to go on a back burner for now.

He was already in the ward when Holly arrived, and he seemed annoyed at her lateness.

'Sorry,' she said. 'I got caught up a bit.'

'You're here now anyway.'

Ryan's tone was cool and he looked away as soon as Holly caught his gaze. 'Let's get on with it, shall we? We've got a lot to get through.'

The administrative meeting he'd just attended was probably responsible, Holly decided. While they kept their private and professional lives as separate as possible, he seemed far more distant than normal.

But his smile for Taylor Johnson, the boy who'd been speared with the tree branch, was as warm as ever.

'You can go home tomorrow,' Ryan told him. 'And back to school next week. Try and stay out of those trees for a while, though.'

'I'm never going to climb trees again,' Taylor assured his surgeon.

'Never say never,' Ryan advised. 'You just need to be careful. Have you still got the stick?'

'Yeah. I'm going to take it to school for news. It'll be wicked!'

Seven-year-old Hannah was still waiting for the surgery to correct the narrow portion of her aorta. That threat of a viral illness had meant postponement until it became obvious that the runny nose and cough were just a mild cold, and a dose of bronchitis or even pneumonia was not going to complicate recovery from her operation.

Holly listened to the girl's chest carefully but was able to voice her satisfaction.

'Completely clear,' she told Ryan. 'Do you want another chest X-ray done?'

'No.' He turned to Hannah's parents. 'We'll go ahead in the morning, then.'

Hannah's mother went pale but nodded bravely, and Ryan smiled at her. 'We'll keep her in the intensive care unit for a day or so after the surgery. I'll get Holly to take you up there now so you'll have an idea of what to expect.'

'Now?' Holly was dubious. It was normal practice to introduce parents to ICU staff and let them see how their child might look if they were on a ventilator or being intensively monitored because being prepared made it that much easier to cope with such a traumatic experience. But there were still several patients to see on the ward and Holly always accompanied Ryan on his rounds.

'Now,' Ryan repeated. 'I'll carry on here and you can catch up through the notes when you get back.' His gaze flicked back to Hannah's parents. 'I'll see you in the morning before we head off to Theatre.'

And with that he was gone and Holly was left with the disturbing impression that something significant had changed. She tried to shake it off.

'Do you want to go and watch TV for a little while, Hannah? I'm going to take Mum and Dad for a visit upstairs.'

'I could draw you another picture, if you like,' Hannah offered. 'Did you keep that lion one?'

'You bet. I've got it stuck to the front of my fridge.'

'What would you like this time?'

'How about a black panther? To go with the lion?'

'Cool. I'll have it finished when you get back.'

* * *

Sue welcomed them into the unit.

'We'll take very good care of Hannah,' she promised. 'She'll have a nurse with her the whole time.'

'Are we allowed to stay with her as well?' Hannah's mother was looking around at all the machinery with obvious misgivings.

'Of course. Let me show you the cubicle she'll be in and the kind of monitors you can expect to see around her bed when she comes back from Theatre.'

Sue let them stop and talk to the parents of a child who was still on a ventilator. In the event that Hannah could need support like this, talking to other parents facing the same ordeal was the best help she could offer. Sue stepped back and raised an eyebrow at Holly.

'I had a visit from Ryan a little while ago.'

'Oh?' Sue's tone warned Holly that she might not like what she was about to hear.'

'He wasn't happy.'

'Oh.' She hadn't been imagining things during the ward round, then. And if Sue was telling her in this kind of tone, it was safe to assume that Holly was responsible for whatever it was that Ryan wasn't happy about.

'He found out that you'd put your name down for the fun run. Did you ask someone about sponsorship?'

'Yes, but I told them not to say anything to anyone. I said that I was a surprise entrant. Nobody is supposed to know who the black panther is.'

'I know. Someone must have squealed, though. Ryan came in here and demanded to know if it *was* you. I'm sorry, Holly, but I couldn't lie. I had to say yes.'

'I wouldn't expect you to.' Holly hadn't lied to Ryan either, so why did she *feel* as though she had? 'What did he say?'

'That you hadn't thought it through properly and I'd better take your name off the list.'

'What?'

Hannah's parents had seen enough so there was no excuse to stay in the unit or any further opportunity to talk to Sue, but Holly was more than a little upset.

Shades of the anger she had experienced on the day she had discovered Ryan had been planning the kidney transplant and talking to doctors behind her back resurfaced and magnified. By the time she entered the ward again, Holly was quietly seething. She could have anticipated him being over-protective and ready to do his best to talk her out of her plan to participate in the run, but to try and control her life like this was simply unacceptable.

This was huge. The annoyance of him checking whether she was being compliant in taking her medication was nothing. Even the difference in viewpoints regarding Holly's desire to have her own baby faded into a category of something that could be sorted out. But this! Ryan had taken on the role of a parent. One of control. Removing her right to make an independent choice and thereby removing her from a position of equality in their relationship.

There was no question of just giving in because she loved him. Yes, she loved him more than she could find words to describe, but fighting for her independence was ingrained. It was as much a part of her as her love for children or her determination to become a skilled surgeon. If she gave in and let it go, she would be denying who she was. She would also be shoving an issue under the carpet that couldn't fail to reappear and potentially destroy anything she and Ryan might build together.

Ryan clearly hadn't anticipated the level of confrontation his action had generated. The look he received from Holly made his eyebrows rise but then he frowned and looked away—a not very subtle reminder that their professional and private lives were separate.

He tapped the set of notes he had beside him on the central desk in the nurses' station.

'I thought you might want to review the procedure we'll be doing on Hannah tomorrow.'

Holly stepped closer and nodded briskly. Fair enough. A personal discussion could wait until they got home. Ryan had opened the notes to find the recorded image mapping the abnormality in Hannah's cardiac vessels.

'The coarctation is located just distal to the origin of the left subclavian artery. We'll do a left posterolateral thoracotomy through the fourth intercostal space. What nerves will be involved with the retraction of the medial pleural flap?'

'Vagus and recurrent laryngeal nerves.'

As soon as Holly's attention was caught by following the outline of the surgical technique she knew she could cope with the tension between them, and there was relief to be found in that knowledge. Keeping things professional at work had definitely been a very sensible arrangement.

They weren't at work the moment they drove out of St Margaret's staff parking lot, however, and even the few minutes of stony silence with which they had walked from the building and climbed into Ryan's car to start the drive home had been unbearable. Holly couldn't wait any longer.

'Just what the hell did you think you were doing, Ryan?'

'Sorry?'

'You know perfectly well what I'm talking about. You told Sue to take my name off the fun run register.'

'Don't you think it should be me asking *you* what the hell you think *you* were doing by putting your name down in the first place?'

'If you had asked,' Holly snapped, 'I would have told you. Trying to stop me doing something without even having the courtesy to discuss it is like a parent trying to control a two-year-old.'

'I had every intention of discussing this with you, Holly. I was confident that you'd see sense and pull out so I thought I'd save you the trouble.'

'Why do you think I put my name down in the first place?'

'God knows,' Ryan said heavily. 'I suspect you're out to try and prove you're capable of doing anything now.'

It was close enough to the truth for his tone to inflame Holly further. The despondency with which she had left the gym earlier that day gave credence to Ryan's obvious belief that she *wasn't* capable, but that wasn't the issue, here, was it? This was about control.

'What if I was?' Holly demanded. 'It's my choice, isn't it?'

'Of course it is. But you can't expect me to stand back and do nothing if I think what you're doing is stupid.'

'Really?' The clipped word was dripping ice. 'If I wanted a relationship with a parent, Ryan, I would have moved in with my father.'

They were stuck in traffic now. It was something that happened virtually every day and normally provided a chance to enjoy each other's company. To talk. Or hold hands even. But right now Ryan's hands were gripping the steering-wheel and his knuckles showed white. And Holly had her arms wrapped tightly around her body.

She was hating this but there was no way out. They were trapped in the car with an almost suffocating atmosphere of conflict. It had to be sorted out.

'What's more,' Holly added, 'my father would be encouraging me to make the most of my life—and health. Not trying to hold me back.'

'I'm *not* trying to hold you back. Your body's under enough strain right now recovering from surgery.'

'That's not stopping you from doing the run.'

'I was fit before I even went into surgery. I'm not trying to adjust to having a new kidney. I'm not taking a bucket of medication.' The points on his list were fired at Holly like spears. 'For God's sake, Holly. You *know* what the odds would be for finding a replacement kidney. Why risk it?'

Holly swallowed hard. Now she knew what had been bothering her so much. 'Would you feel the same way if it was someone else's kidney I was getting used to?'

'What's that supposed to mean?'

'It sounds to me like you still feel some kind of ownership and that gives you the right to dictate what I can and can't do.'

'Don't be ridiculous!'

'*Don't* tell me I'm being ridiculous. I won't let you put me down like that.' Holly's voice had risen and she tried to lower it. 'That's how it feels to *me*. Don't you think I know how important this kidney is better than anyone else? And, yes, we might be together because you gave it to me, but that doesn't give you the—'

'*What* did you say?' Ryan's face was expressionless as he interrupted and turned to stare at Holly. 'What do you mean, we might be together because I gave you the kidney? Did you feel like you owed me something?'

Oh, hell! They had just dived head first into the real issue now, hadn't they? Holly had never seen an expression remotely like this on Ryan's face and it was actually frightening. Her mouth went dry.

'Of course I owe you something, Ryan,' she said carefully. 'You've given me my health back. A new life. But does that mean I have to get your approval for everything I want to do from now on?'

The angry sound of more than one car horn let Ryan know that the traffic was finally moving again. They drove one block and then another in silence. It wasn't until they joined the queue to turn right at another set of traffic lights that he finally broke the silence.

'Let me get this straight. We're together because I gave you a kidney?'

It was what had started everything, wasn't it? Holly couldn't be less than honest. 'I guess so.'

'And is that the *only* reason?'

'What? No, of course it isn't! I love you, Ryan, you know that.'

'But it's what brought us together.'

Holly felt as though she was being somehow derailed. Her thoughts tumbled. Something was going very wrong here. They were heading in the wrong direction. Away from any possibility of having this sorted out before they arrived home and could enjoy the dinner Jack had invited them to.

Holly tried to focus. Ryan's offer of a kidney had been so unexpected. And personal. Of course it had knocked her out of the professional relationship they'd had. It had made her see Ryan very differently. Made her think about him as a man and not just as a surgeon and colleague.

'Yes,' she had to admit. 'It was certainly the catalyst.'

'So, if I hadn't given you my kidney, we wouldn't be together now?'

'I suppose not. But you set the boundaries as much as I did. I never had any idea you might be interested in me being anything other than your registrar. And I was far too sick to think about having any kind of relationship anyway.'

'You started thinking about it, though, didn't you? While you were still sick, I mean. Before the transplant.'

The car was inching forward now and it was almost their turn to move again, but Holly wasn't distracted. She could remember very clearly that first moment when it had occurred to her that she might be falling in love with Ryan—when she had seen his joy having just delivered the breech baby, Sophie. And it had been on the same day she'd known she was also physically attracted to Ryan. That night, when he had taken her home to meet Jack. When she had seen that photograph of Ryan in his fencing outfit and stance. Before the surgery. But after she had accepted his offer.

'You kissed me,' Holly said slowly. 'That night you took me home. Yes, I knew there was the possibility of something happening but I was prepared to ignore it. I suspected it could be a result of the emotional side of the transplant process. I wouldn't have acted on any of it. It was *you* that suggested I come to stay. It was *your* idea to get the tickets to Fiji.'

They were moving again and on a road away from the main routes around the city. Ryan accelerated as they approached a hill.

'So you don't want me telling you what you should or shouldn't be doing on the grounds of it being me that gave you that kidney, is that right?'

'Would you feel the same way if it was an anonymous kidney I'd been given?'

'Yes.' But then Ryan shook his head. 'No.' He sighed heavily. 'I don't know. I suppose I do feel a personal connection. What I *don't* feel is any kind of ownership. I think that impression is coming purely from you.'

Was he right? Holly was silent as Ryan turned again, into the driveway of the old villa this time. Was he simply being protective because he loved her? It couldn't excuse heavy-handed behaviour, though, could it?

Neither of them made any move to get out of the car.

'I think you're with me because you feel that you owe me something,' Ryan said flatly. 'You refused my offer initially because you felt you'd be left with a burden of either guilt or gratitude. It was successful, thank God, so the debt is at least a positive one. I think you could be paying that debt through our relationship. You're with me out of gratitude.'

'No.' Holly shook her head, as much to try and clear her thoughts as deny the accusation. 'I love you.'

'Do you? Are you sure it's not gratitude? That you feel obliged to give me what *I* want because I gave you that kidney? You're already resenting me caring about how you look after yourself.'

Holly's head wouldn't clear. The confusion was getting worse. She *had* been fearful of a debt of gratitude or guilt, but that fear had been associated with a professional relationship. At the time, Holly wouldn't have dreamed of them ever becoming *this* close. Of course she was grateful to Ryan. There was no way she could deny that. The fact that he had been prepared to go through so much on her behalf was a big part of who he was and what she loved about him.

This wouldn't be happening if the kidney had come from an anonymous donor. But if it had, she wouldn't have had the opportunity to get to know Ryan.

To fall in love with him.

It was impossible to separate things. Holly could not take gratitude out of the equation any more than Ryan could remove the vested interest he would naturally have in where a part of his body now was.

By tacit agreement that an impasse had been reached, Ryan and Holly got out of the car and went inside.

Jack must have noticed how quiet they both were during dinner. He said nothing, but for the first time since Holly had met Ryan's grandfather, he looked and moved like the very old man he was. The limits of his time on earth couldn't be ignored.

Neither could the limits that now seemed to hang over Holly's relationship with Ryan. The crunch came when they returned to the other half of the villa.

'I think we both need a bit of space at the moment. I think it might be a good idea if you went home,' Ryan said bluntly.

Holly closed her eyes. She didn't want this. Couldn't bear it. Why had she felt so strongly about taking a stand? Or proving herself? Why on earth had she put her name down for that damned fundraising event at all?

'Is that it? Are you telling me it's over?'

'Is what over?' Ryan asked wearily. 'The payment of your debt? Yes, it's over, Holly. You owe me nothing. I told you that kidney came with no strings and I meant it.' He closed his eyes as he shook his head. 'The only way I can think to show you how much I meant it is to cut whatever strings you seem to think there might be. You're free to do whatever you want with your body, Holly. And with your life.'

Holly fought back tears. She moved to touch Ryan's arm but the muscle felt as responsive as a block of wood. He was determined to take her honesty and twist it into something negative. But how could she persuade him that her feelings weren't an extension of gratitude when she didn't know herself where one emotional response ended and another began?

He was right. She *had* felt resentful at his way of showing concern for her welfare. She *had* felt she was obliged to acquiesce or compromise or hide the complete truth. What sort of a basis for marriage was that?

And what hope did they have if Ryan wasn't prepared to talk about it?

She was being kicked out here,

Punished.

Because she had put her name down for a fun run?

Because she was grateful for what Ryan had done for her?

Nothing had been sorted. The anger that had been with her ever since that conversation with Sue that afternoon was still there. It only needed a tiny stir to spring back into life and, as a self-protection device, it was superb. This wasn't the end of the world by any means. Holly didn't need a pseudo-parent in her life—however attractive he was.

Holly could look after herself. The way she always had done.

'I guess I'll pack my things, then.'

Ryan nodded without looking at her. 'I'll go back next door for a while. Pop hasn't had a game of chess this week.'

'Fine.' Holly's voice was tight. She had offered Ryan all

the love she had and it wasn't good enough, was it? She watched him head back towards the front door.

'I guess I'll see you at work tomorrow.'

'Yeah.' He didn't look back. 'I guess you will.'

CHAPTER NINE

ANGER continued to bubble.

A poisonous brew, like a hot mud pool where bubbles rose endlessly and every so often broke to send droplets that splashed and burned painfully. It had been unfair to direct so much of that anger towards Holly. Ryan knew perfectly well that most of it should have been directed at himself.

The fear had always been there, hadn't it? That he was buying Holly's love by offering her such a valuable gift. He'd been patient for so long, too. Why had it all fallen apart so quickly?

Why couldn't he have resisted the urge to draw Holly closer so fast? To invite her into his home and his private life? And worse—to spirit her away for that romantic, tropical island holiday. He shouldn't have taken advantage of the closeness they inevitably achieved by sharing the experience of the kidney transplant.

At the time, the urge to protect and care for Holly had been irresistible, but that had been at least partly due to the weakening effect of his own surgery. Was that why Holly hadn't objected? Why she had seemed to welcome his attentiveness?

If he'd been thinking straight, he could have seen it had been totally the wrong timing. He should have left Holly alone to recover and regain her health and independence. He might have intended his gift to be made with no strings, but it had been he who had created them, hadn't he? Not Holly.

There was no going back now. He'd destroyed what they did have by acknowledging his fear. He'd tried to bury the fear with anger and he had hurt Holly. Possibly irreparably. She had every right to be angry. But wasn't it better for this to happen now than before they became even more deeply involved with each other?

Neither of them could ever know whether Holly would have fallen in love with him if he hadn't given her that kidney. The debt of gratitude would always colour their relationship and Ryan would always wonder if that had been the only reason Holly had chosen to be with him.

He couldn't live like that. Not knowing. A marriage with that kind of insecurity could never be good enough for either of them. But he didn't want to live without Holly in his life.

It was tearing him apart.

Having to work so closely with Holly wasn't going to make things any easier. Ryan glanced towards the silent figure beside him, scrubbing her hands meticulously in preparation for the surgery to correct Hannah's coarctation of the aorta. Holly was staring at the lather she was creating with the scrubbing brush.

If she turned sideways enough to catch his glance, maybe he would see something in her eyes that would provide a light at the end of the miserable tunnel he had plunged into last night.

A pinprick would be enough. A sign that Holly would welcome a chance to talk. A way to open the door that had somehow slammed shut between them last night and, if nothing else, a way back to the time before the transplant when working together and sharing a love for their jobs had been a joy in itself. Maybe then they could find a way to start again.

But Holly stood on the foot control to release a stream of water to rinse her hands.

She didn't turn her head.

For the moment, anyway, that door appeared to be locked and Ryan had no idea whether a key for that lock even existed. Or whether he should start looking for it until they'd both had some time to think.

He was still angry.

Holly hadn't dared turn to meet the stare she knew Ryan had directed at her while they'd scrubbed up. She hadn't been able to bear to see the accusation that she loved him for the wrong reasons and that those reasons were not enough to build a future on.

Why did it matter so much? Did Ryan think that if the kidney failed a few years down the track, she would instantly *stop* loving him? What mattered was that she *did* love him and that should be enough, regardless of the catalyst.

Then again, what if his attitude was justified? It was what that unrecognised worry had been based on, wasn't it? The fact that Ryan had given her the kidney and had that vested interest in its welfare gave him power that had the potential to come across as being controlling. Holly couldn't live with someone else deciding how she would live her life.

Little things like taking pills or how much exercise or study she did.

But big things, too, like whether or not she had her own child.

And no matter how strongly Holly felt about issues like

that, in the end she would always have to compromise according to Ryan's preference because the unspoken would always be there.

She owed him.

Big time.

A debt that could never be repaid except by loving him and trying to ensure *his* happiness. And if Ryan's happiness had to come at the expense of her own, then the partnership could never be equal and resentments would build and be waiting to explode. They would spend their lives together stepping through a minefield.

No wonder Ryan thought it wasn't good enough.

It wasn't.

Despite her utter misery at the thought of trying to live without Ryan in the personal part of her life, Holly was aware of a curious relief in having the issue out in the open. The biggest mine had been detonated already. All that remained to be seen was whether enough of those fragments could somehow be put back together again to make a whole.

If, somehow, a way could be found past what seemed an impenetrable barrier.

The surgery on Hannah marked a new and rather unwelcome form of professional interaction. Maybe others didn't notice any difference because Holly and Ryan had been very careful to keep their personal lives private. Everybody knew about the kidney transplant, of course, but Sue was the only one who knew what had developed between them since.

Ryan sounded just the same, appreciative of everybody's input, cheerful and eager to share his knowledge and teach others as he worked, but Holly could feel the wall between them. He seemed so distant. The connection was broken.

'Here's where the area of coarctation is,' Ryan pointed

out, as he carefully dissected the vessel free from surrounding tissue. 'There's the left subclavian artery and we're going up the arch. I'm going to tie off the ductus and artery branches and then ligate the ductus. Can you see what I'm doing, Holly?'

'Yes.'

'Put a clamp across the aortic arch between the left carotid artery and the left subclavian artery.'

'Here?'

'Yes. Good.'

Even Ryan's praise seemed distant. So professional. Aimed at the action, not the person.

Holly clamped off the vessel at the top and then at the position Ryan had requested, below the abnormality. She watched in fascination as he cut into the vessel, exposing the defect and cutting it out. Then the repair work began.

'Do you know why I'm using polydioxanone sutures, Holly?'

'They've been shown to provide a secure suture line and allow for growth.'

'Absolutely right. Go straight to the top of the class, Dr Williams.'

An appreciative chuckle could be heard from other members of the theatre staff but the quick glance Holly risked revealed none of those crinkles at the corners of Ryan's eyes. He wasn't smiling.

The warmth had gone.

It broke Holly's heart to see it appear for others. The smile and reassuring hand clasp for Hannah's parents after the surgery had been completed. The easy banter with colleagues as a group from Theatre headed to the cafeteria for lunch.

'So how's the training going, Ryan?'

'Not bad.'

'Are you going to let someone else win this year?'

'Can't afford to. My drug company sponsorship will double if I cross the finish line first out of the St Margaret's contingent.'

'So will mine,' the anaesthetist, James, confessed. 'Guess I'll have to hope you trip over your tail.'

'Tail?' Someone was laughing.

'He's going as a lion. Cardiology's got a wild animal theme going.'

'Always knew you lot were wild.'

With the date for the fun run getting closer, it was only natural that it was such a popular topic of conversation but the reminder of what had sparked the separation from Ryan was too much for Holly. She dropped back from the group, deciding to go elsewhere for her lunch.

Doing a U-turn, Holly headed for the automatic vending machine that contained sandwiches, fruit and drinks. Poking coins into the slot, her attention was caught by the huge new poster on the wall. The blood bank was clearly desperate for donors. A 'Please Spare a Drop' campaign had been started and the huge red drip shape of the poster was certainly eye-catching.

Ryan had always been a regular blood donor but had he responded to the current campaign? The thought made Holly wince. He couldn't afford to give blood until he was completely recovered from his surgery. Not that she would tell him that, of course. Well, she might have suggested it if they had still been talking to each other, but she certainly wouldn't go to the blood bank and tell them he hadn't thought it through and they'd better not take any of his blood if he *did* offer. Wasn't that the equivalent of what he'd done regarding the fun run register? Holly would have more respect for Ryan making his own choices than that.

Her own choice in this matter was an easy one. One of these days she might be able to make a valuable contribution thanks to her blood type. But not yet. She didn't need Ryan, or anyone else, telling her that giving blood would be no more sensible than getting pregnant could be until her body had adjusted to its new state of health.

A few months of looking after herself might make things very different. A good diet. Plenty of rest. An exercise programme. Holly eyed the healthy salad roll and apple she had purchased from the machine but didn't feel hungry. She could do with putting her feet up for a rest, thanks to having had so little sleep last night, but that seemed like a defeatist way to spend her lunch-break.

She might feel as flat as a pancake but the notion of rolling over and admitting defeat was anathema. Maybe exercise was the answer. It was becoming a front-line treatment for depression, wasn't it? There didn't seem much point in pushing herself to join the run any more but it would be pathetic to give up a fitness programme. Especially having forked out what had been a rather expensive membership at the gym.

The decision was easy to make. Holly moved swiftly to her locker, where she abandoned her lunch for the moment and collected a bag that contained her old T-shirt, shorts and a pair of trainers.

'I'll just do some weights today,' she told Janine when she got to the gym. 'I haven't got much time and I don't really feel like running.'

The effort of getting there had been worthwhile. The

small glow of satisfaction was enough to lift her spirits. Time with the children on a ward round that afternoon helped as well, probably because Ryan had been called away to assist the other cardiac surgical team with a major operation. The positive effect dissipated rapidly, however, when Holly arrived home at her apartment that evening.

The rooms still felt cold and empty and had that odd smell of a house that hadn't been lived in for some time. And the plants were all dead. Holly hadn't noticed that when she had returned in the dark the previous evening. She'd had other things on her mind, anyway. But now the contents of the pots couldn't be ignored. They seemed symbolic. Accusatory. The few leaves still clinging to twigs were as wilted as Holly's emotional well-being.

Perhaps tomorrow would be better. Being Saturday, it would be more relaxed with no Theatre session and only a ward round before she had the rest of the weekend off. They were not on call. Ryan might not be so angry. He might even apologise and Holly could let go of her own anger at what seemed blatantly unfair treatment. They could talk to each other and try and find a way to repair the damage inflicted.

But the next day was a rerun of the day before in the polite professional stakes and that irked Holly. *She* hadn't done anything wrong. She hadn't dismissed Ryan's feelings for her as being in any way unworthy, had she? It had been Ryan who had decided that what she had to offer wasn't good enough so it was up to him to make the first move and apologise. If he actually wanted to put things right, surely that's what he would do?

The minefield was still there.

'Morning, Holly,' Ryan had said at the start of that day. 'How are you?'

The tightness of the accompanying smile had advertised all those mines. How was she feeling? Had she taken her pills? How was that kidney behaving?

'I'm fine, thanks,' Holly had answered. And her smile had been just as tight as his.

Thank goodness for the time off. Holly headed for the gym before she went home and this time she found herself eyeing the treadmill as she used other weight machines.

'May as well give it a go,' she muttered. The reduction of her anti-rejection medication was still having positive effects. Physically, at least, Holly was feeling good.

Managing nearly five minutes of a gentle jog was a boost. And Holly still had enough energy to stop her sitting around with too much time to think when she got home. She cleaned her apartment. She went to the supermarket to stock up on groceries. She did her laundry and planned how to use her Sunday.

Another visit to the gym was first on the list. Then a shopping trip to a garden store to purchase some new plants and fresh potting mix. And a visit with Sue was well overdue. Holly needed her friend right now. She was missing Ryan. And Jack. If she stopped being busy for more than a few minutes, the lonely sensation just pulled her down.

Sue's tiny house was in a leafy suburb in one of the older parts of Auckland. With her husband and three children sharing the cottage, it was crowded and noisy and so homely it made Holly's heart ache to see so clearly what was missing from her own life.

Cake baking had been in progress and the children all had chocolate smears around their mouths and sticky fingers clutching spoons as they wrangled over licking the mixing bowl clean.

'Right. That's enough.' Sue swooped on the bowl and slid it into the hot water filling the sink. 'Outside, you lot. You can all go and help Dad weed the veggie garden.'

'But we're helping with the cake!'

'Yeah.' Lucy, the eldest took over as spokesperson. 'We have to make the icing now.'

'The cake's got to finish cooking first,' Sue said firmly, 'and then cool down. *Then* we can make icing. Right now, Holly and I are going to have a coffee and some grown-up time. If *any* of you set foot in this kitchen before the timer on the oven goes off, you won't get to eat a crumb of it.'

Mutinous mutterings emanated from the children as they headed for the back door.

'And put your gumboots on,' Sue called after them. 'It's muddy out there.' She grinned at Holly. 'What's the bet I have six mud-caked shoes to clean before I go to work tomorrow?'

'Want me to check whether they're putting them on?'

'Nah.' Sue flopped into a chair at the kitchen table. 'I want you to talk. You look miserable.' Her smile was sympathetic. 'This is about Ryan, isn't it?'

Holly nodded sadly.

'So he hasn't apologised?'

'No.'

'Has he tried to talk to you at *all*?'

'Only about work stuff.'

'Have you tried to talk to him?'

Holly shook her head again. 'The right opportunity never seems to come up and I have to say I haven't gone looking for one. I can't exactly go and grovel and ask him to take me back, can I?'

'Of course not. He'll see sense, Holly. Just give him a bit of time.'

'That's what I keep telling myself. And that's another reason I can't make the first move. If he does love me enough to want to marry me, he'll do something to sort things out. And if he doesn't love me that much, it wouldn't be much of a marriage, would it?' Holly's gaze drifted to the window where she could see the children hopping in a freshly turned patch of soil—no gumboots in sight.

'Things will work out.' Sue smiled at Holly confidently as she got up to pour the coffee. 'The problem is that you're both surgeons. You both want to make the decisions regarding someone's care and there's a little switch in your heads that won't allow you to relinquish control.'

'You're saying *I'm* the control freak?'

'As far as your own health goes, yes. I've never seen anyone so determined and in control. How are you feeling, by the way?'

'Fabulous,' Holly said dryly. 'Physically I've never felt better in my life. I ran for eight minutes at the gym today.'

'Wow!' Sue set down the mugs of coffee. 'You'll be able to do the run with us after all, then. I never did take your name off the register.'

'Ha!' Holly rolled her eyes. 'That'd go down well, wouldn't it? Ryan would never speak to me again.'

'Why not?'

'It's what started this whole fight.'

'Remind me why you were so mad about it?'

'Because Ryan tried to stop me doing it.'

'And you didn't want to be stopped, right?'

'Right.'

'So why are you letting him stop you now?'

* * *

Why indeed?

Holly was still replaying the conversation with Sue in her head as she drove home. If she didn't attempt the run and she and Ryan did end up sorting things out, wouldn't she always wonder if that sorting out had been successful because she'd given in and done what Ryan had wanted? How would that help anything?

If she did run and Ryan accepted the statement she was making, then the opposite would be the case, and if they sorted themselves out they would have a solid base for an equal partnership.

And if she did run and they never got back together, at least she would know she could still meet a difficult challenge and get through it. Therefore, she would be able to keep meeting other difficult challenges in her life.

Like getting over Ryan and getting on with her life.

It wasn't entirely coincidence that she met Ryan at the costume shop a couple of days before the run. They shared pretty much the same schedule so it made sense to use a gap on Thursday afternoon to ensure they collected the supplies they needed before the shops ran out.

Many thousands of people took part in this annual run. The entry fee they paid went to the general charity supported, but large groups of people—like the St Margaret's Hospital staff—also collected separate sponsorship for their own fundraising projects. Not everyone dressed up, but as representatives from a large children's hospital it always seemed appropriate to provide some entertainment to the children who would be lining city streets to watch.

Ryan had a large bundle of shaggy, tawny fur in his arms

when Holly arrived at the shop. He stood back, seemingly checking out the display of face paint and other accessories but also watching silently as Holly collected and paid the hire fee for her pile of sleek black fur.

'Do you want any face paint?' the salesgirl asked.

'Yes, please.' Not that there was any point in trying to disguise herself any more, but if she was going to do this, she may as well go the whole hog.

'So you're still going to do the run, then?'

Holly had to stop and meet the stare directed at her from Ryan.

'Yes… I am.'

The eye contact seemed welded into place. Neither appeared willing or able to look away. Unspoken messages flashed between them. Ryan was taking this as confirmation that his opinion counted for nothing. Holly was reiterating her right to make her own choices. There was a hint of hurt bewilderment on both sides as well.

How had it come to this?

Hadn't Ryan told her—way back—that he admired her courage and determination and independence? Why would he now want to stifle those attributes?

Questions.

But no answers.

It was Ryan who broke the eye contact and turned away.

'Good luck, Holly.'

Luck might well be needed.

It was one thing to have been so determined and put so much into her training, but quite another to see the size of the event she was about to participate in for the first time.

Getting dressed at Sue's house had been fun. The black

panther suit could have been designed to show off Holly's height and slim build. Sue's husband had given a very appreciative whistle.

'Cut that out,' Sue had ordered. 'You're supposed to be rounding up dwarves, not ogling the panther.'

Sue's youngest child, three-year-old Ben, had kept pulling off his long bobble hat and sitting down in the middle of the chaos.

'He'll never walk that far,' Sue had told Holly, 'so I'm going to be in the pushchair brigade. Are you walking or running?'

'Running,' she had said confidently.

But now she wasn't so sure. There was an air of anticipation at the beach start venue that was surprisingly nerve-racking. Along with the media vehicles and police cars on the nearby road were three ambulances. Did they expect a lot of problems? It had only been last year, hadn't it, that a run in another part of the country had produced a fatality? A young man had collapsed and died of a heart attack only seconds after crossing the finish line.

Maybe Holly should join the walkers rather than the runners. She could go with Sue and the people pushing young children or in wheelchairs themselves—they were gathering on the road surface rather than the sand. But then Holly spotted a lion and she knew it was Ryan because he was talking to James, the anaesthetist, who had a Superman outfit on. And she thought of the support that had snowballed when word had got round the gym she had been attending so often in the last couple of weeks. Complete strangers had offered to sponsor her and she stood to make a significant contribution to the fundraising all by herself if she completed the run.

Holly joined the runners but kept to the back of the huge group watching the massive organisational task being undertaken. They would be released in stages according to projected speed. Runners first, then walkers—many of whom were accompanied by children or dogs. The ones with wheels came after that along with a medley of those just out for fun, sporting roller blades, skateboards, unicycles and scooters. She could even see a couple of people on stilts.

A brass band was playing, cans of coins being shaken as people collected donations from spectators and shouting and laughter came from all directions among the thousands of participants. No wonder they had chosen a small cannon to signal the start of each section.

It took a long time for all the runners to pass through the flags. Being near the back of the group, it was several minutes before Holly found she had enough space to start jogging. She couldn't see where Ryan and the other St Margaret's staff were and she didn't expect to see them again until after the finish when they were due to meet up for a celebratory barbecue. Ryan and James would be right at the front of the pack in any case, competing to double their fundraising efforts by being first across the line.

Holly settled into a moderate jogging pace and was delighted to find herself actually passing others. They ran along a road section of a couple of kilometres and then there was another part of the beach included on the route. This time the sand felt like glue on Holly's feet and the effort began to tell. She could feel herself slowing and her heart rate increasing as she pushed herself on.

There would be no shame in walking for a stretch, she reminded herself. And she would have done precisely that except it was at that point she spotted a lion to one side and not far ahead.

There had to be more than one person dressed like that. It couldn't be Ryan. The leaders were at least a kilometre or more ahead of Holly by now. But then the lion turned its head and Holly knew it *had* to be Ryan. He was giving up the chance to keep his status as the fastest and fittest member of St Margaret's staff and the extra money in order to keep an eye on her. Why else would he be so far back in the pack? And why else would his head keep turning in her direction?

There was no question of slowing to a walk now. No way. If Ryan wanted to watch her fail so that he could say 'I told you so', he had another think coming.

They hit the road again and Holly increased her speed. It was much harder to breathe now and she was aware of an odd buzzing sensation in her head, but they were well over the halfway mark. She would probably see the finish line around the next bend or so.

Spectators were thin at this point and the road wide enough to allow a television station van to roll alongside, filming the event. An ambulance, its lights flashing, was coming up behind the van. Somebody up ahead must have injured themselves. At least it wasn't *her* being rescued. She turned her head, wondering if Ryan was still watching and might be thinking the same thing.

She couldn't see him, which made her keep looking, running with her head turned, ignoring the pain in her chest as she struggled to pull in enough oxygen to keep her legs moving. People around were shouting but that odd buzzing muted the sounds so Holly couldn't tell whether it was encouragement or something else.

She gave up looking for Ryan. It was all Holly could do now to keep putting one foot in front of the other. To keep moving.

And then something hit her. Hard. Holly was propelled sideways at speed and had no hope of regaining any balance. She bounced off one runner and then straight into another, who somehow caught her as they both fell. It all happened so fast Holly had no idea what could have happened. Had she tripped? Or accidentally got in someone else's way?

'I'm sorry.' Holly pushed herself to her hands and knees as other runners bypassed the obstacle she made with the runner who had cushioned her fall. 'I'm *so* sorry.'

'You bloody *idiot*!' The voice came from behind Holly. 'Just look what you've *done*!'

Holly looked, still on her hands and knees, still gasping for breath. But she could make no sense of what she saw.

The ambulance, its beacons still flashing, had stopped. So had the television van and a police car. Just in front of the ambulance was a pile of what looked like tawny-coloured fur.

'You weren't even looking where you were bloody *going*!' the stranger's voice accused Holly. 'You went in front of the van and almost right in front of that ambulance just when it was picking up speed.'

'That guy saved you,' someone else informed Holly. 'If he hadn't pushed you out of the way, you would have been run over.'

'And *he* got hit instead.'

Holly fought a wave of dizziness and nausea as she kept her gaze on that tawny heap.

It wasn't moving.

Ambulance officers were crouching beside it now and they were looking grim.

Holly struggled to her feet and staggered towards the scene. She couldn't get close enough because there were too many people trying to help now so she stood gazing helplessly at the ominously still figure lying on the road. Voices around her sounded disembodied.

'He just threw himself in front of us. There was no way we could have seen him!'

'Is he breathing?'

'Can't tell under all this damn fur. Grab some shears. And some oxygen.'

'Keep those cameramen out of here.'

'Get a neck collar. If he's not breathing it could well be a cervical injury.'

'Would someone, please, move those spectators out of the *way*?'

Holly felt someone catch her arm. 'Come this way.'

She wrenched her arm free. 'No way!' Holly turned to the police officer trying to clear the area and gave him a defiant stare.

'I'm not going anywhere,' she announced. 'I'm staying right here with Ryan.'

CHAPTER TEN

'THIS lady knows the lion.'

Holly was pushed closer to Ryan and a paramedic looked up.

'His name is Ryan Murphy,' she said shakily. 'He's a doctor.'

'Ryan?' The paramedic leaned close and pinched an ear lobe. ' Dr Murphy? Can you open your eyes?'

There was no response.

Another paramedic was sliding a neck collar into place and fastening the straps. A second ambulance rolled up and stopped.

'Any medical conditions we should know about?'

'He had a kidney removed about two months ago.'

'What for?'

Good question. Holly fought back a wave of pure misery and her voice caught. 'So he could give it to me.'

The lion suit was being unceremoniously sliced down the front.

'Fractured right femur,' one of the crew announced. 'I'll get a traction splint.'

'Bruising to the abdomen, left side, possible rib fractures,' another said.

'Good dent to the back of his head as well, on the right side.' An oropharyngeal airway was being inserted into Ryan's mouth to protect his airway and then an oxygen mask hid his features.

Holly was trying to absorb the information she was hearing. A fractured femur on the right. A possible splenic injury and fractured ribs on the left, an occipital blow to the right side of the head.

A classic car versus pedestrian multi-trauma injury. For children, anyway. Common enough to have its own name. Waddell's triad. An adult would normally be too tall to collect these injuries but Ryan hadn't been standing upright when he had been struck, had he? He'd been diving forward to push her out of the way so the top of his leg could well have been at bumper level, the fender hitting his lower ribs and then the road surface being responsible for the head injury.

It added up to a nasty set of injuries, capable of producing severe blood loss.

'Let's load and go,' a paramedic ordered. 'We'll get IV access established on the road.'

A traction splint was applied to Ryan's broken leg and then he was log-rolled onto a backboard because of possible spinal injuries. Foam cushions held his head immobilised, strapped into place. Larger straps held his body to the bright orange board. Within a commendably short period of time, the board was lifted to a stretcher and then into the back of an ambulance.

'You coming?' a female paramedic asked Holly. 'Are you a friend?'

Holly simply nodded and climbed the steps. The back doors slammed shut behind her and someone thumped on the outside of the doors to give them the all-clear to head away. Holly could hear the muted sound of the siren and through the small, square windows on the back doors she could see crowds of people continuing the fun run.

This was as far from fun as Holly could imagine. She watched the paramedic crew as they worked on Ryan. She saw the first needle penetrate a vein on his arm and she could remember so clearly the day she had taken that blood sample for Ryan. How *alive* his skin had felt. Had *that*, in fact, been the first recognition of how attracted she was to him?

Or had it really been so long ago she couldn't put a specific date to it? Could only remember how lovely she'd thought the first smile he'd given her had been.

What did dates matter, anyway? Nothing mattered apart from the fact that Ryan was badly hurt. And it was her fault. This hadn't been the first time Ryan had risked his life for her, but this time it had been due entirely to her pig-headedness.

She *was* a control freak.

Ryan wasn't.

How could she have ever doubted that his actions had stemmed from a genuine concern for her?

From love.

He hadn't been running that close to her in order to see her fail and rub her nose in it. Knowing Ryan's personality, the notion was just plain insulting. Just as insulting as accusing him of trying to retain ownership of the kidney. And she'd had the nerve to feel self-righteous. Angry. She hadn't given him a chance over the last couple of weeks, had she? He wasn't going to make the first move when he could have faced rejection. He'd been unsure of the strength of Holly's involvement and, instead of reassuring him, she had made things worse by stamping her foot and going ahead with her plans to prove her physical capabilities.

And he had still been there for her. Trying to stay close enough to watch out for her. To support her.

Holly was still in a dazed state of self-recrimination when they arrived at Auckland General's emergency department. She only took in snatches of the handover.

'GCS of 7.'

'BP's dropped. Narrow pulse pressure. Currently 80 over 60. We've run in a full litre of saline.'

'Closed fracture of the right femur.'

'Abdominal distension, left side. Rib fractures.'

Holly had pulled the head of her costume back to hang down but she felt ridiculous, standing in this high-tech resuscitation area wearing an animal suit. Ryan had been stripped of any vestige of his costume but Holly couldn't see the body of a patient who might have further injuries that needed assessment.

She could only see the familiar, solid shape of the man she loved.

'What's that scar from?'

'A nephrectomy.'

'What did he need that for?'

'He didn't. He was a living donor, apparently. For that panther.' The ED consultant looked up and smiled at Holly. 'Is that right?'

She nodded.

'Any complications with the surgery?'

'No.'

'Any other medical history we should know about?'

'No.'

'Allergies?'

'Not that I know of.'

'Airway's clear.' The doctor at the end of the bed adjusted the oxygen flow. 'Saturation's down. Ninety-two per cent. Breathing's shallow. Respiration rate of 36.'

'We need another line in. Get some bloods off at the same time for a type and cross-match.'

'He's O negative,' Holly told them.

'Isn't that the one the blood bank's extra low on?' a nurse asked.

'Find out,' the consultant ordered. 'And order some packed cells and fresh frozen plasma. I'm not happy with the level of hypovolaemia.'

'And I don't like these oxygen saturation levels,' the doctor in charge of Ryan's airway and breathing announced. 'I think we should intubate and get him onto a ventilator.'

Holly had to step back as the level of activity around Ryan's bed increased. X-rays were ordered and taken. A CT scan and abdominal ultrasound booked. More blood tests were done and a surgical consultation requested from both general surgery and orthopaedics. A neurosurgeon was called to look at Ryan's head injury.

Jack arrived at the hospital half an hour later.

'What's happening, lass? Is he badly hurt?'

Holly nodded and then burst into tears. 'This is all my fault, Jack.'

The old man's arms felt stick thin but their grip around Holly was firm. 'That's enough of that,' he comforted gruffly. 'It'll be all right, love, you'll see. Ryan's a tough old bird, like me. He's not going to die.'

But Holly wasn't so sure about that.

The way things were looking right now, losing Ryan on a permanent basis was a horrific but definite possibility.

And that prospect was, quite simply, unbearable.

Pain.

Through a dark mist, Ryan was only aware of having the worst headache of his life. Mercifully it faded and his next awareness was pain in his leg. That, too, seemed to fade and a more familiar ache took its place. He'd felt this one before. When he'd had that kidney removed.

Holly.

Awareness of her filled the darkness, overwhelming any physical considerations. Fear stepped in. Holly had been in terrible danger. He couldn't remember why, but the desperate need to *do* something was paramount. He struggled to move. To open his eyes.

'Take it easy, son. Everything's all right. You need to rest.'

No. Everything *wasn't* all right.

'Pop?' Ryan couldn't recognise the odd croak that seemed to be his voice. He had to blink and concentrate on trying to focus his vision.

'It's me,' Jack confirmed. 'I'm here, Ryan.'

'Where?'

'You're in the intensive care unit, lad. You got yourself a bit mashed up.'

'How?'

'You got smacked, don't you remember? By an ambulance, of all things.' Jack's chuckle was strained, as though laughter had only just won over tears. 'Not a bad idea, that's what I say. If you're going to get run over, you may as well choose a vehicle that can help pick up the pieces.'

Ryan didn't care what had hit him. Or what injuries he

might have sustained. There was something far, far more important he needed to know. With a mouth as dry as the Sahara and a thickened tongue, it was too hard to get more than one word out at a time, but a single word was all he needed.

'*Holly*?'

There was a tiny pause. A hesitation that hung in the air as Jack gave his hand a reassuring squeeze. Ryan could hear the beep of a monitor falter as his heart skipped a beat. Why did he need reassurance? What had happened to Holly that Jack was reluctant to tell him?

He managed two words this time. 'Tell me.'

'She's been admitted to hospital. I've been to see her a few times. She's asleep just now.' Ryan's hand received another squeeze. 'They reckon she's going to be all right, son. She's just needed a spot of dialysis to help her along.'

Oh, no! The kidney had failed.

His dream had failed. Instead of being able to spend the rest of his life with the woman he loved, he would be sentenced to watch her slowly die. He didn't bother trying to open his eyes again. Why hadn't that damned ambulance done a better job of running him over? This was far worse than any physical pain could be.

'She's going to be all right,' Jack repeated firmly. 'And so are you, thank God.' He cleared his throat. 'And thanks to Holly, of course.'

Ryan pushed the lead weights of his eyelids up again. 'Why?'

'You were at death's door, lad. The bump on your head isn't so bad but you broke your leg and you needed to have your spleen taken out. You lost way too much blood and they didn't have enough of the good stuff to give you. There's some crisis in the blood bank at the moment apparently. Anyway, you weren't looking so good this time yesterday, let me tell you.'

There was a connection here that Ryan wasn't getting. He felt lines in his forehead gather as he frowned. 'And?'

'And Holly insisted on giving you some of her blood. One unit was OK, they were happy enough to let her do that, but it wasn't enough and Holly insisted on giving you more.'

'*No-o.*' The word was halfway between a sigh and a groan. How could Holly have put herself at risk like that? A major blood loss was a dangerous strain even on a healthy body. On a system that was still adjusting to something as big as a new kidney, it could be devastating. How could any responsible doctors have allowed her to take a risk like that?

His thought must have been obvious.

'She insisted she felt fine,' Jack explained. 'She got another doctor on her side. Doug somebody? Anyway, she gave this speech to your doctors. Said they would never find a better match and she demanded the chance to help. She said…' Jack had to clear his throat twice this time. 'She said she loved you and she was prepared to take whatever risks were associated with giving you more blood. She argued some medical stuff about them giving her some packed cells or something to replace her blood and that you needed the whole blood far more than she did.'

'And they *let* her?'

Jack was smiling. Ryan could focus well enough now to see the tear that tracked a tortuous route down the deep wrinkle lines on his grandfather's face.

'She was pretty damned persuasive. And she did seem fine. She sat in here with you all night. It was this morning that she fell over. They've given her all kinds of stuff. They said the dialysis is just to try and give that old kidney of yours a bit of a rest.'

Ryan shook his head. 'Not my kidney,' he said. 'Holly's.'

'You need to rest again, too.'

Ryan had no option. He was being pulled back into that dark place, his mind and battered body under the control of medication.

'Tell Holly...I love her.'

'I'll do that, lad. I think she knows, mind you. And I'll tell you something else. She loves you. You're a lucky man.'

Indeed he was. Holly loved him. She had risked her life to help him. Nobody did something like that simply from gratitude. How could he have ever doubted the strength of that love? It didn't matter a damn what had precipitated them finding each other. The only thing that mattered was that they belonged together.

For ever.

Ryan managed an approximation of a smile. 'I know.'

'Sleep well, lad.'

'You've been very lucky, you know that, don't you?' Doug Smiley wasn't smiling at the moment. 'Don't scare me like this again, young Holly.'

'I won't, I promise.'

'I'm going to hold you to that.' The older physician did smile now. 'Want some more good news?'

He'd already given her the rundown on her vastly improved condition so more news had to be about someone else. Holly caught her breath and sat forward eagerly. 'Ryan?'

'He's looking great. Going to be moved out of ICU and into the ward later today.'

'Can I see him?'

Doug's smile widened. 'Just don't go exchanging any more bodily fluids for now. Or any other bits and pieces that happen to take your fancy. You two have shared quite enough.'

A kiss didn't count as exchanging bodily fluids, did it?

Not the gentle one that Holly bestowed on Ryan's sleeping lips anyway.

Or even the much firmer, longer one when Ryan opened his eyes and reached to pull Holly back well within kissing distance.

Holly's legs felt wobbly enough to make her sink to the chair positioned near the head of Ryan's bed but she couldn't give up the physical contact. Both her hands were linked with his. She took a deep breath.

'I'm sorry, Ryan. It's my fault this happened.' Having started, the words tumbled out. 'You were right. It was a stupid thing for me to try and do. I was out to prove something and I was too thick to realise that I didn't need to prove it at all.'

'You shouldn't have done it, Holly. You've got no idea how worried I was.'

'I know. I am sorry. I'll follow Jack's advice from now on. I won't run before I can walk properly.'

'I wasn't talking about the run. I meant that you shouldn't have risked your life giving me so much blood.'

'But I had to!'

'Really? From what I've heard, you put up one hell of fight to be allowed to do it at all.'

Holly just smiled. When Ryan raised his eyebrows to suggest that he still wanted an answer, she responded with a question instead.

'What was the real reason you gave me your kidney?'

It was his turn to take a slow inward breath. To measure his words.

'Because I love you,' he said softly. 'I had to do something to try and help you survive because I felt like I was watching you die by inches and a part of me was dying right along with you. The most important part. My heart.'

Holly blinked back tears. 'Same,' she whispered. 'That's exactly the same reason I had to give you my blood.' She sniffed inelegantly. 'Only you were trying to die a lot faster than I did.'

'I won't do it again.' Ryan's grasp on Holly's hands tightened. 'I haven't even said thank you.'

'You don't need to. I wanted to do it. It was my choice. You don't owe me anything, Ryan Murphy.'

He smiled. 'Same,' he murmured.

A whole minute ticked past and then another as they simply held each other. With their hands. And their eyes. Holly could swear their souls were touching as well.

'I love you,' she whispered.

A gleam of mischief made the gold flecks in Ryan's eyes sparkle. 'Same,' he said. Then he relented. 'I love you, too, Holly Williams. More than I could ever say.'

Holly's eyes were wide enough to make her look appealingly innocent. 'You're good at leaving offers open, aren't you, Ryan?'

'Such as?'

'Oh, I don't know. Kidneys, bacon and egg sandwiches—that sort of thing.'

'Yeah, I guess I am.'

'So…that other offer you made? Is it still open?'

Ryan's face was a study in blankness. 'What offer?'

'Oh, you know. The one to marry you. To live with you for the rest of my life. To have a family and stuff.'

'Oh…' The twinkle made it obvious that Ryan had been deliberately obtuse. He had known exactly what Holly had been about to ask. Maybe he'd just wanted to hear the words.

'Oh, *yes*,' he said with utter conviction. 'That offer is most definitely still open.'

'In that case…' Holly did her best to sound suitably solemn but joy was taking control of some of her muscles. Her mouth was insisting on curling into the biggest smile ever. 'I'd like to accept your offer, please.'

Recovery for Ryan took longer this time. A period in which Holly and Jack became very close as they shared caring for him. Being such a vital part of the household seemed to give Jack a new lease of life.

'Every cloud has its silver lining,' he announced. 'That's what I say. Never had so many games of chess in my life!'

It was Jack's old restaurant overlooking the sea in one of the most beautiful bays in Auckland that Ryan and Holly chose as the venue for their wedding reception three months later, on Christmas Eve. It was Jack whom Holly chose to give her away.

'Not that I'm giving anything away,' he whispered loudly, right in front of the altar. 'Keeping you in the family, that's what I'm doing. As you should be, lass.'

Keeping that kidney in the family as well. A kidney that continued to perform as perfectly as if Holly had been born with it. Apart from having to take her anti-rejection medications, she was in perfect health. Holly found more than enough stamina to study for and pass the rigorous examination process that saw her become a fully qualified surgeon the following year.

Jack, at ninety-seven now, was still beating Ryan at the occasional chess game. Turning Jack into a great-grandfather when he was ninety-eight was not planned, but when Holly found herself pregnant both she and Ryan were unanimous in their decision to accept what life had chosen to throw at them, to deal with whatever risks were involved and to be grateful for any joy that also came their way.

So much came that the name of their daughter was decided the moment she arrived in the world and was pronounced perfectly healthy.

They called her Joy.

Holly's kidney had coped with the strain of pregnancy. And it continued to perform with no hint of her body trying to reject it.

'Of course not,' Ryan said more than once. 'Why would it? It was a perfect match after all.'

And Holly had a favourite rejoinder.

'Just like us.'

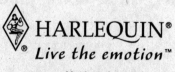

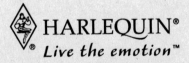

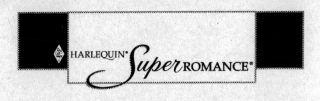

…there's more to the story!

Superromance.
A *big* satisfying read about unforgettable characters. Each month we offer *six* very different stories that range from family drama to adventure and mystery, from highly emotional stories to romantic comedies—and much more! Stories about people you'll believe in and care about. Stories too compelling to put down.…

Our authors are among today's *best* romance writers. You'll find familiar names and talented newcomers. Many of them are award winners— and you'll see why!

If you want the biggest and best in romance fiction, you'll get it from Superromance!

Emotional, Exciting, Unexpected…

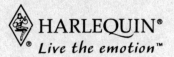

Harlequin Historicals®
Historical Romantic Adventure!

From rugged lawmen and valiant knights to defiant heiresses and spirited frontierswomen, Harlequin Historicals will capture your imagination with their dramatic scope, passion and adventure.

Harlequin Historicals...
they're too good to miss!

SILHOUETTE *Romance*®

Escape to a place where a kiss is still a kiss...

Feel the breathless connection...

*Fall in love as though it were
the very first time...*

Experience the power of love!

Come to where favorite authors—such as

Diana Palmer, Stella Bagwell, Marie Ferrarella

*and many more—deliver modern fairy tale
romances and genuine emotion,
time after time after time....*

*Silhouette Romance—
from today to forever.*

Live the possibilities